Battle of the Hexes

A Paranormal Women's Fiction Cozy Mystery

Season of the Witch
Book 3

Shéa MacLeod

Battle of the Hexes
Season of the Witch – Book 3
Text copyright © 2022 Shéa MacLeod
All rights reserved.
Printed in the United States of America.

Editing by Alin Silverwood
Cover Design by Mariah Sinclair (mariahsinclair.com)

The characters and events portrayed in this book are fictitious. Any similarity to real persons, living or dead, is coincidental and not intended by the author.

No part of this book may be reproduced, or stored in a retrieval system, or transmitted in any form or by any means, electronic, mechanical, photocopying, recording, or otherwise, without express written permission of the publisher.

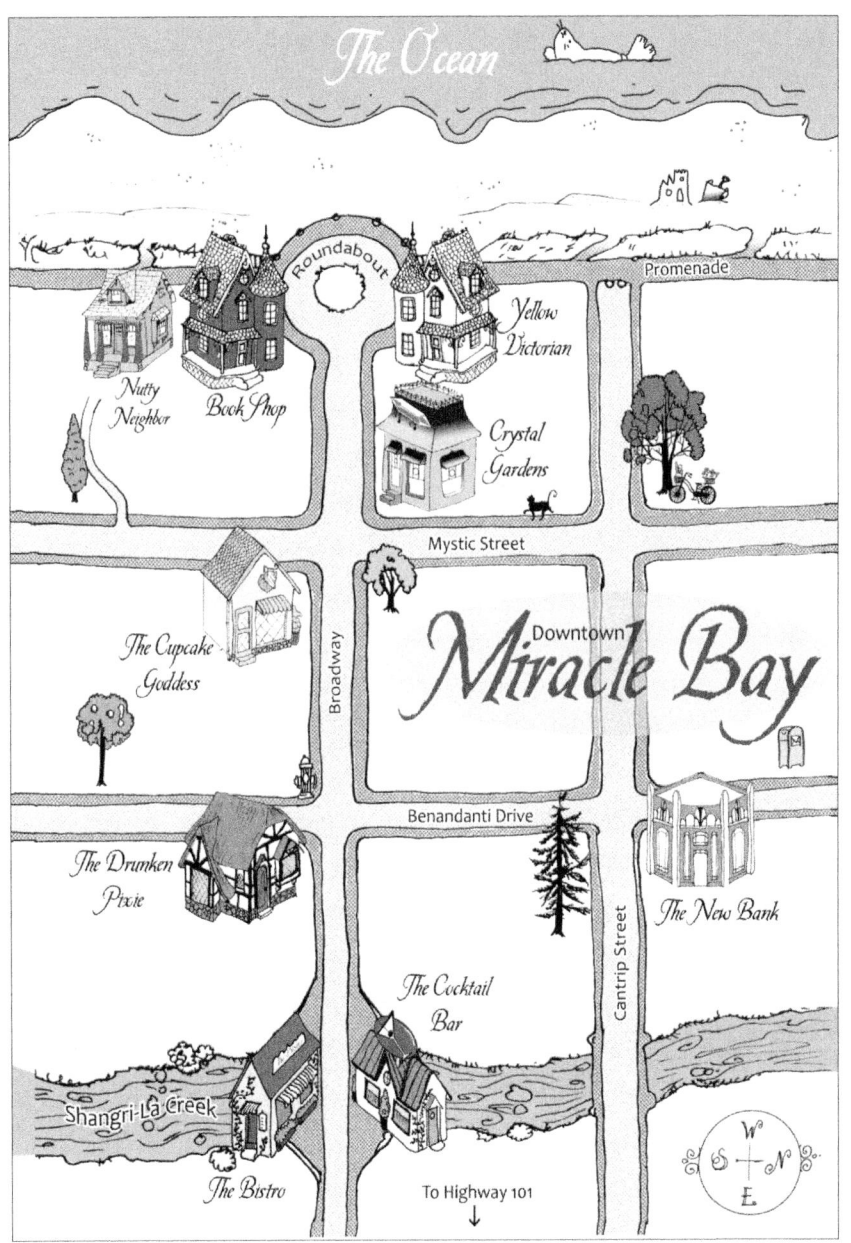

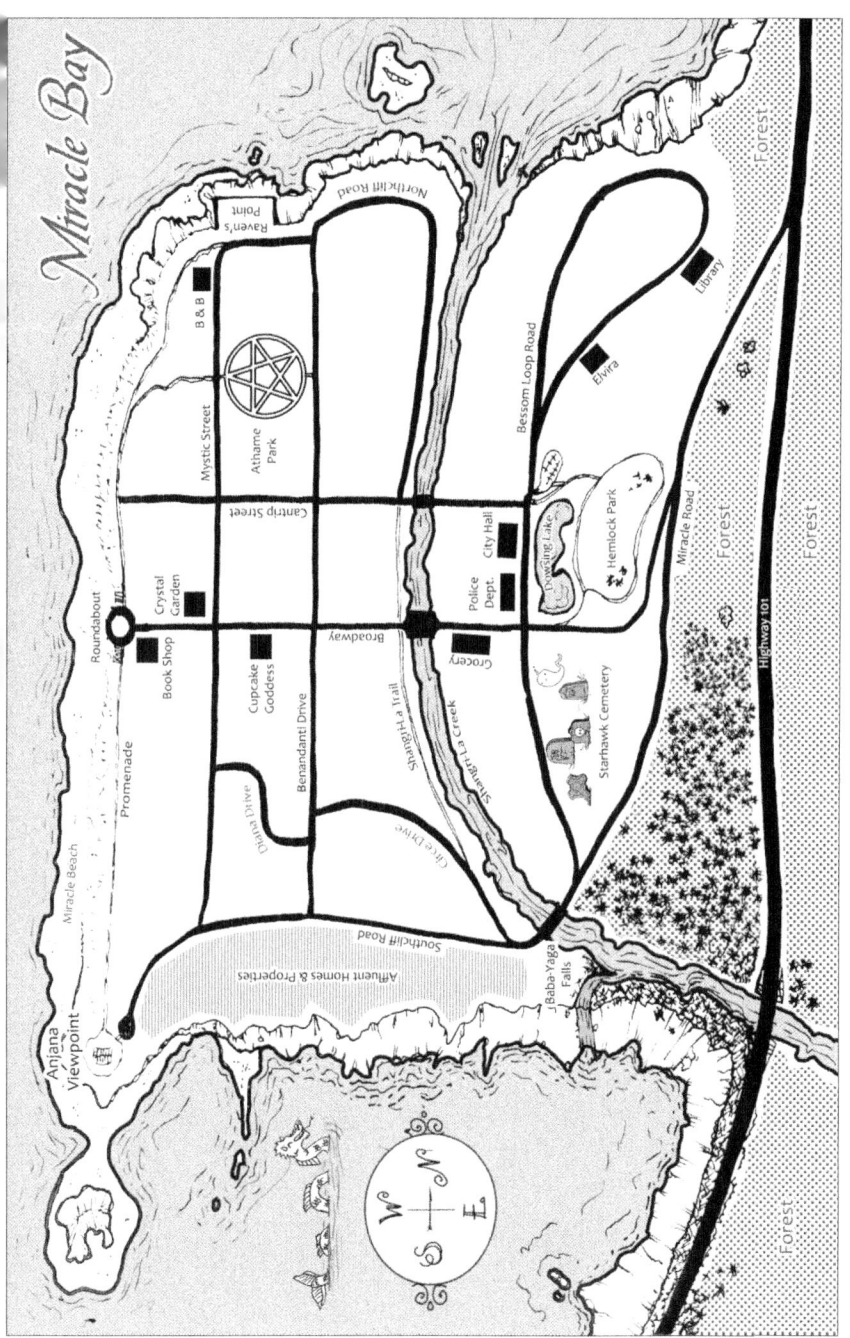

Dedication

For Amy, who would 100% be on board for witchy cocktails, but who definitely wouldn't help me turn anyone into a frog. Probably.

one

I hadn't meant to turn my ex-boyfriend into a frog, but here we were.

Honestly, if there was such a thing as Karma, Kenneth would be a horny toad. Emphasis on horny.

In any case, there he stood—or rather squatted, or whatever it is frogs do—on the top step of the front porch of my shop, Belle's Books and Candles (and Coffee). He stared at me out of large, bulbous eyes. I stared back, convinced I was hallucinating. Afraid I wasn't.

His throat bulged. "Ribbit."

"Don't you 'ribbit' at me. It's not my fault you're a frog. Okay, it is, sort of, but you have to admit part of this is your fault." He was, after all, the one who dumped me. On my birthday. For another woman.

It had been upsetting at the time. Well, maybe "upsetting" is too mild a word. After all, I'd been upset enough my latent magic raged out of control and the results were currently on my porch.

"Ribbit." The frog's tone was snide. Typical Kenneth. He took snide to a whole new level.

"Fork." I rubbed my forehead. I was suddenly getting a headache.

"What is it?" Emerald Merriweather, my best friend, asked as she came up beside me, a box of homemade candles clutched to her chest. "Oh, look. A frog. How…cute?"

"That's not a frog," I said. "And he's not cute."

She gave me the side-eye. "It sure looks like a frog."

"Trust me, it's not," I assured her. I noticed she didn't press the cute issue.

"Then what is it?"

"My ex."

She blew a lock of emerald hair out of her eyes and shifted her grip on the box. "You dated a frog?" She sounded incredulous.

"He wasn't a frog at the time." Maybe I should rephrase. "He wasn't *physically* a frog at the time."

"Oh, right. He's the one you turned into a frog."

"Not on purpose," I muttered.

She set her box on one of the chairs gracing the wide wraparound porch of the massive Victorian. Emerald's main gig at the shop was reading tarot, but she had a side business making and selling candles both for ritual use and for fun. Based on the strong scent of cinnamon and the green color, the box held abundance candles. "How can you tell it's him and not just some random other ugly frog?"

"Ribbit?" Outrage this time.

"How many frogs do you know wear bowties?" I pointed at the garish red and yellow paisley.

She squatted down. "Is that what that is? Goddess, that's an ugly tie. Suits him. How did he get into Miracle Bay?"

"Your guess is as good as mine."

Miracle Bay was a small town on the Oregon coast, pretty much like every other town on the Oregon coast except for one thing: everyone who lived there was magical. Including yours truly. And because of that, the town was hidden from view via a spell. If you didn't have magic, you didn't get in. In fact, you couldn't even find the town. Not unless you knew somebody who could get you through the spell. But here sat Kenneth—albeit in frog form—over a hundred miles from his home in Portland—and *inside* the mystical fog barrier that protected Miracle Bay from non-magical humans.

Emerald stood up and crossed her arms, her long, emerald skirts swishing against her bare legs. It was an unseasonably warm morning for spring. "Your ex isn't magical, is he? Like maybe a low level wizard or something?"

"Kenneth? Not that I know." We'd dated before I knew I was a witch with actual magical powers. He'd dumped me for another woman, one he claimed was more sophisticated and better suited to his needs. On my birthday. I'd sort of lost it, which was how he got turned into a frog.

It had taken me a while to realize that a) Kenneth was now a frog, and b) I'd been the one to hex him into one. Before I could catch him and attempt to turn him back, he'd disappeared. Then I'd inherited my grandmother's bookstore, moved to Miracle Bay, and forgot about the whole thing.

That's a lie. I occasionally felt a stab of guilt over the frog situation, but since there hadn't been a lot I could do about it, I'd shoved it out of my mind. In my defense, I'd had a lot on my plate, what with figuring out how to use my magic, learning how to run a business, and solving my grandmother's murder. Frankly, it had been pretty easy to pretend the whole Kenneth incident hadn't even happened.

"If he's not magical, then how'd he get here?" Emerald pressed. "Could someone have brought him?"

"Who? And why?" I frowned at the frog on my doorstep. How would anyone know this frog was really a bespelled man? Other than the bowtie, that is. And especially who would know that *I* knew this frog? That *I'd* hexed this frog. Man. Whatever.

Emerald sighed. "I don't know. Could be a coincidence."

I snorted. "Heck of a coincidence."

"True," she admitted.

At that moment, the frog turned around, leapt off the porch, and disappeared into the bushes.

Without thinking, I dashed after him, shouting, "Don't let him get away!"

"Oh, great," Emerald sighed. "Here we go again."

"Come on! Stop dilly-dallying!" I dashed down the steps and along the strip of land that led to the backyard.

"Did you seriously just use the term 'dilly-dally?'" Emerald puffed along behind me, her footsteps silent in the grass. "What are you? Eighty?"

I wasn't. I was forty-six, but I spent a ridiculous amount of time with an eighty-something-year-old, learning magic and how *not* to blow stuff up. An unfortunate side effect of my abilities and one I hadn't totally mastered.

The frog who was definitely Kenneth dodged out from under a shrub and disappeared beneath one of my grandmother's raised herb beds which was in dire need of weeding. I wasn't much of a gardener. Ducking my head beneath the plywood bed, I reached for Froggy Kenneth, but he hopped at the last minute, and my lunge turned into a scrabble followed by a backpedal.

"Ow!" I smacked my head into the underside of the bed. "He's headed for Rhodore's yard. Get him!"

Rhodore had been my neighbor but was currently incarcerated in magic prison for murdering a fellow supernatural and using toxic, forbidden ingredients in his face creams. Yes, I know it sounds insane. You're not wrong.

There was a screech of metal as Emerald opened the gate between my backyard and Rhodore's. "I can't see him."

Drat. Had he gotten away?

I scrambled from beneath the herb bed and, rubbing the sore spot on my head, hurried to Emerald's side. In the month or so since Rhodore had been hauled away to the paranormal pokey, his lawn had grown out of control, and the weeds stood almost waist high. There was no way we were going to find a frog in that jungle. At this point, Froggy Kenneth could be anywhere."

The back door of the seafoam green Craftsman banged open, and a woman stood on the back porch squinting at us. "Can I help you?"

"Um—" My brain fritzed out.

"Um—" Emerald repeated with equal intelligence.

The woman was unusually tall, close to six feet. She looked to be about fifty, lushly rounded with an overabundance of curves, and long, yellow-blonde hair that tumbled to her butt. She had a rose tattooed along her lower leg so that the leaves and brambles twined around her calf. But that wasn't what sent us speechless.

Never mind the fact it was spring, and despite the warmth of the day the breeze off the Pacific Ocean held a distinct chill. Never mind the fact that two perfect strangers were standing in the middle of her yard gawping at her.

My new neighbor stood there, hands on hips, buck-ass naked.

two

I'd never seen so much naked boob in my life.

"Can I help you?" the new neighbor repeated, giving a luxurious stretch. Her voice was rich and low, and she drawled her words out as if she was in no hurry.

"Um," Emerald said, unable to take her eyes off my nudist neighbor.

"I-I'm your neighbor," I finally blurted, pointing behind me at the Victorian rising above the hedges. "I own the bookshop."

"Oh, how nice. I love books." She strolled languidly down the back steps, boobs jiggling so violently I was afraid she'd give herself double black eyes. The weeds whipped at her bare legs, but she didn't seem to notice as she walked toward us. "I'm Dahlia Wildes. I just moved in. So good to meet you." She grabbed my hand and gave it a forceful shake.

"I'm Juniper Jones, but everyone calls me JJ. This is my friend, Emerald Merriweather."

She shook Emerald's hand with equal enthusiasm.

"I'm sorry. We didn't mean to interrupt," I said.

She blinked. "What do you mean?"

I waved a hand up and down to indicate her lack of clothing. "I guess you were... uh, taking a bath or something?"

Taking a bath? Seriously, sometimes my brain and mouth weren't connected.

Dahlia let out a hearty laugh that sounded dangerously close to a donkey bray. "I'm a Green Witch," she said, as if that explained everything. Maybe it did, but not to me. I was too new to the whole witch thing.

"What does practicing Earth magic have to do with being naked?" Emerald asked the question foremost in my mind. I was glad I wasn't the only one confused.

Dahlia guffawed again. "Clothing puts a barrier between us and the energy flowing through the universe, don't you think?" She waved her arms in wide circles, as if to embrace the universe. How did she not have backaches?

"No," said Emerald a little tartly. "Energy flows through me just fine when I'm clothed, thank you." She smoothed a hand down her trademark green skirt as if afraid our nudist neighbor might try and rip it off her.

I tried really hard not to snicker. I was only marginally successful.

"How about you?" Dahlia turned wide hazel eyes toward me.

"Um, I mostly stay clothed, too." I wasn't about to admit I had no idea what sort of witch I was. That was something I was still figuring out.

Dahlia sighed. "Don't tell me I've landed in yet another Puritanical town."

I bit my lip so hard I nearly bled. "Not at all. We just expect people to wear clothes, generally speaking—especially when in public—but this is your property now, so you do you." And now I would be prepared for a naked witch next door.

"Really? None of you dance skyclad?" She looked crestfallen.

I glanced over helplessly at Emerald. "We mostly drink cocktails."

"It's nice today, but most of the time it's too cold and drizzly for skyclad," Emerald explained. "Plus, not everyone is comfortable with it. So mostly... yeah, cocktails."

"Oh!" Dahlia clapped her hands in delight. "I do love a cocktail."

"I'll let you know next time we do any cocktail magic," I said. Hopefully she'd wear clothes. I wasn't sure the health department would appreciate a naked witch anywhere near the bookstore's cafe. If there was a health department in Miracle Bay. "Well, it was nice meeting you, but we're, uh, in the middle of something." I wasn't about to admit we were chasing a frog. It sounded insane, even to my ears, and even when compared to a nudist Green Witch.

"Busy, busy," Emerald said cheerfully, giving my new neighbor a little wave.

"Stop by any time!" Dahlia watched us retreat back through the gate before striding through the grass toward the dilapidated shed that had once housed Rhodore's lab.

I wondered how she planned to use it. Hopefully she wouldn't be brewing illegal potions like her predecessor.

"What do we do now?" Emerald asked as we took the back steps and I let us into the Victorian's kitchen. It now housed the coffee shop/cafe. "Latte?"

"Sure. I'll grab your candles."

While I retrieved the abandoned box of candles from the porch, Emerald whipped up a couple of lattes. She was always trying new flavors and combinations, and today's was white chocolate and cardamom. Since cardamom was one of my favorite spices, I approved.

Sliding onto one of the barstools along the coffee shop counter, I took a sip. "Mmm. Delicious. I'm not familiar with cardamom's magical properties."

"There aren't many," Emerald said, giving me a sly look. "But most agree that its most potent effect is love."

I nearly choked on my coffee. "Excuse me? I do not need a love potion."

She laughed. Unlike Dahlia Wildes's bray, Emerald's laugh was delightfully sunny and warm. "It's true. The way Con looks at you, I don't think he needs help."

My cheeks heated to molten lava levels, threatening to bring a hot flash with them. Conrí Byrne was an enforcer for the local witch council and Miracle Bay's answer to the FBI crossed with a bounty hunter, only a lot more dangerous. He was a wolf shifter, gorgeous as heck, and we'd been on a couple dates. I wouldn't call him my boyfriend just yet, but things were going well. So far.

I took a deep breath, trying to ease the tingling in my fingers. My magic flared in response to hot flashes, and that's when things blew up. I did not need to destroy another coffee machine. Especially one that cost several thousand dollars.

Emerald grinned. "Don't worry. It's also used for relaxation, clarity, and eloquence. Besides, you know I don't have your skill for infusing beverages with magic, so the effects would be mild at best."

I took another sip. It was true. Any witch could add ingredients to a cocktail to enhance it. Even add a little spellwork. But my gift was apparently far rarer. My cocktails were actually magical. Just like my grandmother's had been. She'd had other abilities, too, but the jury was still out on whether I'd inherited those.

"What do we do about Froggy Kenneth?" Emerald changed the subject.

I swallowed a mouthful of latte. It really was delicious. It would probably be very popular. "I don't know. I need to catch the little bugger so I can unfrog him."

"He doesn't seem to want to cooperate."

"No," I admitted. I was somewhat surprised by that. Why wouldn't he want to get turned back to a human? "I'm still curious about how he got here. I mean, it's a long way to hop for a frog."

"Did you tell him you were moving to Miracle Bay?"

I frowned, dredging up the memory of that dreadful date. "No. I didn't get the letter from the lawyer until I got home that evening. Kenneth was already a frog by then."

"Could he have followed you home and overheard or something?"

I shook my head, draining my mug. "The letter only asked for a meeting. I didn't learn about the town or my inheritance until later. I definitely would have noticed if a frog tagged along to the attorney's office."

She twirled her mug between her hands. "So how'd he know to come here?"

I shrugged. "Beats me."

"Unless somebody brought him."

"Makes the most sense. But why? And how'd they know he was not only bespelled, but that I'd done it?"

"Maybe they didn't. Maybe it's a coincidence."

We exchanged looks, then in unison said, "Naw."

"Which begs the question, what exactly is going on?"

"I don't know." Emerald took both of our dirty mugs and set them in the sink. "But whatever it is, I doubt it's anything good."

The rest of the day moved quickly. There was a new Stephen King novel out, and several people had pre-ordered it. Plus, with the new fantasy TV series that just started streaming, there was a run on everything epic fantasy. And, of course, the usual suspects stopped by for their weekly fixes of caffeine and reading material.

There was a short lull around lunchtime, so I brought down Biddy McGraw's journal. She was my many-greats-grandmother—I'd lost track of exactly how many—and her handwritten diary was filled with anecdotes, recipes, and general musings about life and witchcraft. If there was anywhere I could find something about how to unfrog Kenneth, it would be in Biddy's journal.

Unfortunately, the closest thing I could find was a spell to unburn toast. I supposed that could come in handy, but it was probably easier to just scrape off the burned parts with a butter knife.

Somewhere in the early afternoon while I was ringing up a stack of romance novels for one of my customers, a man walked in. He was a stranger to me, but I didn't think much about it since I was still pretty new in town.

He was good looking, but in a saturnine way. He wouldn't look out of place in a dark cloak, creeping through a forest, doing nefarious deeds. His eyes were creepy, dark wells, but I barely had time to notice them.

"Can I help you?" I called as he peered around the shop.

He sauntered to the register. "The statue. When was it built?"

I frowned, handing the bag of books to my customer and bidding her goodbye. "Sorry, what statue?"

He grimaced. "The one at the end of the street."

"Ah. That statue." I glanced out the window overlooking the beach. Broadway ran straight through the middle of town, ending on a roundabout overlooking the ocean. In the center of the roundabout was a gold statue of Branwen, Welsh goddess of love and beauty and one of the founders of Miracle Bay. She now ran a cupcake a shop. "As far as I know, it's been here as long as the town has. So a couple hundred years or so." Probably more. I was never really clear on the exact date. Most people thought Astoria was the oldest Oregon town. They'd be wrong. "Why do you ask?"

But it was too late. He was out the door, striding toward the statue. How bizarre.

First a frog, then a naked neighbor, now this guy. What was going on? Was there a full moon or something?

I walked over closer to the window and watched as the stranger circled the gold statue, bending over to inspect it, then stretching to eyeball its head. After giving it a good once over, he stood back, hands on hips. I couldn't see his expression, but his posture screamed frustration. What the heck was he up to? Why was he so into Branwen's statue?

Just then, another customer entered. By the time I was done helping them, the stranger was gone. I gave a mental shrug and went about my day. There were all sorts in Miracle Bay, and none of them were exactly typical.

By the time I shut up shop at 6:00 p.m., I was beyond exhausted. Emerald had finished her readings a couple hours earlier and had already gone home, so it was just me. I flipped the sign to "Closed" and was about to lock the front door when I saw Kenneth the frog sitting in the middle of the road, staring at me.

I wrenched open the door and Kenneth took off, hopping down the street away from the ocean toward the center of town. I tore off after him, my ballet slippers slapping against the pavement. He was a fast little frog; I'd give him that. Almost preternaturally so.

Without warning, he veered off down a side street, and I followed, my breath heaving out of my lungs and sweat pouring down my face. I was already getting a stitch in my side.

"Kenneth, you idiot," I puffed. "I'm trying to help you."

He either didn't hear or didn't care because he squirmed under a fence and disappeared. I'd have followed, but I was afraid if I took another step I'd fall on my ass.

I was rescued as my phone merrily pumped out the new *Wonder Woman* movie theme song. I pulled it out of my jeans pocket and stared at the screen a beat.

It was my mother.

Now don't get me wrong. I don't hate my mother, but she's... a difficult woman and she should have probably never been a mom to begin with. She's a free spirit—a little too free—and is usually off jaunting around the world with whatever random guy most recently rang her bell, if you know what I mean. She rarely returns my calls and never, I mean never, calls me first. Something had to be wrong.

"Mom?"

"Why are you so out of breath, darling?" She sounded as easy breezy as usual.

I ignored her question, asking one of my own instead. "What's wrong?"

She laughed. "Does something have to be wrong for a mother to call her daughter?"

The answer was yes, since that was the truth, but I found myself shrinking back into my old doormat habits. Don't upset Mom. Don't rock the boat.

"Of course not. I just—I mean—"

"Goodness, darling, you sound a mess. You really need to learn to be more decisive."

My fingers started tingling, and I clenched them into fists as I slumped onto the curb beneath a streetlight. Breathe in. Breathe out. I focused on the building across the street which had cute little planters out front full of petunias. The tension in my shoulders eased. "Sure. Of course. How are you, Mom?"

"Oh, wonderful, darling. Just marvelous. I'm in Prague. Isn't that delightful?" She tittered a laugh.

I blinked. "Prague?" Last I'd heard she was in Paris. Or was it the cruise? It was hard to keep up.

"Of course. I met this simply marvelous man in the Louvre. Simply gorgeous." She lowered her voice. "And rich, darling. So rich!"

"Um, good for you?"

"Don't be snide, Juniper. It doesn't suit you." Before I could protest, she barreled on. "Have you sold that ridiculous house of your grandmother's yet?"

"No, Mother, I haven't. Don't you remember? I told you I'm keeping it."

There was a beat of silence. "Nonsense. That was just a phase. You must be practical."

That was rich, coming from her. "I am being practical. This is a successful business."

"Which is why you should sell it, darling. You know nothing about business."

I frowned. She was right. Or rather, she was right once upon a time, but I was learning. And this is what my grandmother—both my grandmothers, Agnes and Elvira—

wanted for me. To be successful, independent, to love my life and revel in my magic. But of course, I couldn't tell Mom about magic. For all her airy bohemian, fairy ways, she wasn't into anything she considered "woo woo."

"I'm not selling the bookstore, Mom." I hoped that would be final, but I should have known better. My mother might be flighty, but when the mood struck, she could be as stubborn as a stuck record.

"Don't be ridiculous, Juniper. The entrepreneurial life doesn't suit you in the slightest." There was a sipping sound. No doubt she was enjoying her favorite martini. She never strayed far from the classic. Unlike me. I enjoyed experimenting, trying new recipes and flavors.

"How do you know?" My tone was sharper than I intended. It annoyed me that she always stuck me into a box. I wasn't allowed to be or do anything that went against her image of me. One of practicality and, well, bland boringness. I closed my eyes and took a deep breath. "I've never tried it before. I might be good at it."

She gave an incredulous laugh. "Don't be daft, darling. You're like your father. Lovely man, but very dull and not at all adventurous. It takes gumption to run a business darling. *Gumption.*" The indication being that neither my father nor myself had it.

I caught myself grinding my teeth at her disparagement of my father and tried to remind myself she had loved him. In her way. That was another problem with my mother. It all boiled down to *in her way,* and her way wasn't necessarily very kind to the rest of us. Her way meant the minute my father died ten years ago, she flitted out of my life—with his insurance money in tow—and into a never-ending round of increasingly wealthy suitors. I'd been left to deal with the reality of his estate and getting on without my dad, the one person who'd always loved and looked out for me.

"Did you call simply to disparage my life's choices?" I asked tartly.

"Of course not." She tittered in a way that told me there was a handsome man nearby. "I was simply returning your call. You have been *persistent*." She said "persistent," but her tone said "annoying."

"Oh, right." I'd actually forgotten I'd called her several times since moving to Miracle Bay, not that she'd bothered calling me back. The most recent had been because of some things I'd learned while cleaning out my grandmother's closet and trying to solve her murder. Might as well be blunt. "Why didn't you give me Agnes Jones's letters?"

There was a long pause, then another titter. This time one of discomfort. "I don't know what you're talking about, darling."

"Yes, you do. Agnes Jones—my grandmother, Dad's mom—sent me letters. Many of them over the years. You sent them back unopened and you never told me. You knew she was alive all that time, yet you never told me. You told me she was dead. You *lied* and I want to know why."

three

"Don't be silly, Juniper." My mother's voice sounded tight and strangled. I could imagine her rose-painted lips pressed into a thin line. "I don't know about any letters. Agnes died long before I met your father."

There it was. The lie I'd been told my whole life.

My neighbors across the street—the vampiric versions of the Golden Girls—had told me about the letters Agnes had written me after she'd learned of my birth. They had no reason to lie, but my mother... well, you could never trust my mother. Not really. It burst out of me before I could stomp it down. "You're lying."

"That's uncalled for," my mother snapped. "I don't appreciate your tone, Juniper."

I almost apologized, except I wasn't in the wrong. She'd lied to me. Committed a federal felony, for goddess's sake. And I wanted to know why. "I think it *is* called for. I want to know why you didn't give me my letters."

"This conversation is over." The other end of the line went dead.

I stared at my phone. Part of me was angry and part was shocked. Not only had I not gotten any answers, but I hadn't even gotten the chance to ask how or why Agnes had a photo of my mother when she was young. Supposedly the two had never met, but the picture I'd found had been taken at least a good few years before Mom met Dad, so why would Agnes have it? Everyone back home in Portland thought she was dead, so it wasn't like Dad would have sent it saying, "Hey this is my new wife." If that were the case, he'd have sent their wedding photo.

So many questions, and the one person who might be able to answer some of them was the most stubborn, onery woman on the planet. My mother.

I sighed and shoved my phone back in my pocket. I was certainly failing epically today. There was no point moping about it, since there wasn't much else I could do at the moment. Froggy Kenneth refused to be caught, and my mother refused to speak to me. Goddess save me from divas, amphibious or human.

Heaving myself to my feet, I made my way slowly back to the shop. It sat at the very end of the main street in Miracle Bay—Broadway—right before the roundabout that overlooked the beach and the Pacific Ocean. Isabelle Jones, my ancestor, had founded the town along with Branwen, and had also built the Victorian that now housed my shop. Apparently, she didn't warrant her own statue.

My Victorian was on the south side of Broadway, bordered on one side by the promenade that ran along the beach. The dark wine-red siding was accented with gray and black. A sign out front bore bold letters spelling out Belle's Books and Candles (and Coffee). The shop had been named after my great-great-something-grandmother. Across the street on the north side was an identical Victorian, only it was painted lemon yellow, with blue and green trim and was home to my aforementioned vampire neighbors.

Once inside, I locked the door and clumped my way upstairs. I could use a long soak in the clawfoot tub.

My grandmother's apartment—now mine—was located in the attic. I mostly kept the bohemian decor because I liked it. It suited me, just as it had presumably suited Agnes.

I had just started the water running when a black cat—or what looked like a black cat—twined his way into the bathroom. He elegantly jumped onto the rolled rim of the tub and stared at me out of giant, unblinking green eyes.

"What are you doing here, Enki? I'm taking a bath."

I'm your familiar. Where else am I supposed to be?

The first time I'd heard him speak inside my head in that Alan Rickman voice—complete with British accent—I admit I'd freaked out a little. But apparently everyone in Miracle Bay could hear him, so either it was a mass hallucination, or he really was a talking cat. Er, familiar. Apparently, familiars took on whatever shape suited them or their witches or something. I wasn't sure why he chose a cat, since I was allergic. Fortunately, my cat allergy didn't extend to cat-resembling familiars.

"I don't know," I said, "but you certainly aren't around when I need you. Only when you want to annoy me."

And when have you needed me lately?

"Oh, I don't know. How about when my ex-boyfriend showed up?"

You expect me to, what? Fight some enormous, hairy male? No thank you. That's what you have Con for. He curled his tail around himself and literally turned up his nose.

I ignored the jab about Con. "Kenneth is not an enormous male, hairy or otherwise. He is currently in the form of a frog, as you well know."

I haven't got time to keep track of all your disastrous assignations.

"Yes. Because I have so many of them," I said dryly.

For all I know you've left a trail of frogs in your wake. Don't let yourself prune, he said, hopping off the tub and strutting out the door in the way only cats can. *Most unbecoming.*

"Who asked you?" Unfortunately, my epic comeback fell on deaf ears. Enki had already disappeared.

The following night was spellwork practice at Elvira's. The day had been slow, and there'd been no sign of the frog. If it hadn't been for Emerald seeing him too, I would have thought I'd dreamt it.

Elvira, I'd recently discovered, was my step-grandma. She'd been married to my Grandma Agnes for decades after Agnes had left her husband, my grandfather, and fled to Miracle Bay. Like me, Elvira was a witch. Unlike me, she knew what she was doing. She was also the town librarian and had been since the '50s. She looked like Betty White—Goddess rest her soul—from the fluffy white hair to the colorful track suits.

I walked since it was still unusually warm for spring and hadn't rained in a while. The barrel-shaped planters along Broadway were overflowing with colorful blooms: pansies, primroses, irises, tulips... A riot of fuchsias spilled from baskets hung from the antique iron lampposts up and down the main street of town. The Pixietwists had put a new goddess statue in the window of their shop, Crystal Gardens. She perched among the crystals and ferns, perfectly formed from clay, a crown of flowers made from pink and green crystals ringing her head. Ostara, I was betting.

Further along, Green Witch Gifts—which was really more pot shop than gift shop—had a display of colorful egg-shaped glass bongs with a tie-dye sale sign. I was pretty sure I didn't need one even if they were kind of pretty and 20% off. Branwen's The Cupcake Goddess looked exactly as it usually did, with only the barest nod to spring in the form of a mound of cupcakes decorated with slightly gaudy frosting flowers. Too bad she was closed for the day, or I'd have gotten some cupcakes to take with me.

Elvira lived in a converted Art Deco bank across the street from Twisted Whiskey, a whiskey distillery/tasting room. Which was convenient, seeing as how she'd turned the old bank vault into a speakeasy. It was probably my favorite place in town, especially on nights where magic met cocktails. Which was more often than not.

The building was from the early part of the twentieth century with elegant, clean lines and geometric shapes. Even the double doors were original oak framed in brass. Beside the door was a small plaque that read *Private Residence* and a doorbell, and below that was a keypad.

She'd texted me the code to the door, so I let myself in. It was cool and dark inside, old school jazz floating out from the speakers poked into strategic corners. I immediately felt my shoulders ease down from my ears.

Graceful columns rose from sleek, marble floors, while art deco chandeliers hung from the high ceiling. The teller windows had all been torn out long ago, creating a vast room that had been partitioned off—by bookshelves, silk screens, or whatever else had struck Elvira's fancy—into smaller areas, each dedicated to something she considered essential to the Craft.

One area held a work bench lined with little glass apothecary jars, each neatly labeled in Elvira's spidery handwriting. Massive wooden racks hung with drying herbs and flowers. Bookcases were filled with essential oils, recipe books, tinctures, and other interesting accoutrements. Another area held art supplies and various works, including a half-finished acrylic painting of a fairy circle. There was even a library, completely overrun by overstuffed bookcases and overflowing piles of books.

At the back, a monstrous thick door stood open. A sign next to it that said *Vault*. That was Elvira's speakeasy. I was hoping we'd have our lesson there. Instead, I found her pottering around in her garden section.

The garden area held rows upon rows of raised beds of every herb you could imagine. Full spectrum lights hung over them since there was no way they'd get enough sunlight from the high windows. The air was redolent of moist earth and fresh greenery. Elvira watered the plants by hand since, as she explained, most automatic watering systems would make the air too moist for the books in her library. Plus, she claimed she found it soothing to do it herself. She was bent over what looked like basil, muttering to it. Spellcasting or just talking to her plants? Elvira would probably say it was the same thing.

I cleared my throat to be heard over the music.

Without looking at me, Elvira pointed a black remote at a corner of the room and smashed a button. The volume dropped to something more manageable.

"Hey, G-ma. Giving the basil a talking to?" I teased.

"They're not looking as sprightly as they should," she said, straightening. "I'm giving them a bit of encouragement. I found a new recipe for a cocktail."

"Let me at 'em. I'll get 'em growing." I wiggled my fingers. Anything that involved a cocktail had my interest.

She gave me a look. "Stay away from my basil. Plants are not your forte."

"Hurtful, but true."

She gave one of the basil leaves a final, gentle tap, then turned toward me. "Now, what shall we practice today?"

"Well, I'd like to learn something practical like cleaning the house."

"But?"

"What do you mean but? I didn't say but."

She raised a brow. "It was implied."

I sighed. It was impossible to hide anything from Elvira. "I think we might need a drink for this one."

"That bad?"

"You have no idea."

"Well, then, to the vault."

The only indication that the good-sized room had once been a bank vault was the massive steel door that stood open. One wall was taken up with a rack filled with dozens of bottles of wine. In the center of the room stood a long bar, its wood top polished to a shine, the wall behind it covered in mirrored shelving stocked with vintage glassware and bottles filled with every kind of booze imaginable. There were three plush red velvet high seats at the bar, plus a comfortable loveseat and matching side chairs nearby.

"How about something for clarity?" she asked, taking up her usual place behind the bar while I climbed onto one of the bar stools to watch her work.

"Works for me."

She dumped vodka, lemon juice, limoncello, and a few other things into a Cobbler shaker, gave it a vigorous shake, then poured the fragrant, pale-yellow drink into two coupe glasses. She lifted her glass. "Bottom's up!"

I could feel the tingle of magic at the very first sip. Elvira might claim my cocktails were more powerful, but hers packed a darn good punch.

As we enjoyed our cocktails, I told her about Frog Kenneth's arrival in town and our attempts to capture him. I also told her about my new nudist neighbor, Dahlia Wildes.

"Ah, yes, the council was abuzz about her. We don't often get new people in town, so everyone gets overexcited when we do. She comes from a small private commune on the East Coast not far from Salem."

"What's she doing here?"

Elvira shrugged. "Why does anyone go anywhere? Change of pace? The need for something new? Who can say? Now, about your frog problem."

Here it came.

"You do realize you're the only one who can turn him back." She gave me an expectant look.

"No, I didn't. I figured any witch could undo whatever I did." I honestly had no idea how I'd done it in the first place.

She shook her head. "Only the witch who hexed him can turn him back."

"I don't know how," I said. "I didn't even know I cast a hex."

"Strong emotion and magic run willy nilly can do that," she said, taking a sip of her drink. "But I can help you figure out how to undo the hex. But first—"

"First," I prodded.

"You need to catch him, JJ. It's the only way we can turn him back, and we need to turn him back before it's too late."

"I'm trying," I assured her, polishing off my drink. "He's as slippery as a... Well, as a frog." I eyed her. "What do you mean, 'too late?'"

"The longer he's in this form, the more accustomed he'll become to it. He'll start thinking and acting more and more like a real frog until, eventually, his humanity will be completely gone, and we won't be able to turn him back. He'll be stuck as a frog forever."

Based on the way he'd stared at me and his rude ribbits, I was pretty sure there was no danger of that happening any time soon. "Wait a minute. Does that mean there are frogs running around that are actually people?"

She laughed and dropped fresh ice cubes into the shaker, followed by the other ingredients. Apparently, we were going for round two. "I doubt it. It's a rare power, transmutation, and not one I thought ran in the Jones family."

Well, that was a relief, I suppose. "Don't I get all the luck."

She gave the shaker a vigorous shake, ice rattling against the metal sides. "The real question is, who brought that frog here?"

"Emerald and I wondered the same thing," I said, holding my glass out for a refill. "She suggested maybe Kenneth had magical abilities I didn't know about and got here by himself. I don't think Kenneth has a magical bone in his body, frog or human. Besides, it's too long a distance in frog form."

"No, I agree. It's most likely somebody brought him here, and I doubt it was for any good reason." She tapped one purple nail on the counter. "What about this new neighbor of yours?"

"You said Dahlia came from the East Coast. How would she even know Kenneth?"

"Good point." She squinted. "Internet?"

"I guess it's possible," I admitted. "But then how would she know not only that he'd been turned into a frog and then brought here? I just don't see it."

"I suppose you're right. You should speak to Eoinn."

Eoinn was the resident psychic. I'd met him when I first arrived in town, and he declared we would be "best friends" because he'd seen it. In a vision. I wouldn't say we were best friends, but we'd certainly become friendly and had even hung out a bit.

"I thought he saw too many possible futures to be any use."

"He does," she agreed. "But you don't need to know the future. You need to know the past." She held up the shaker. "Another?"

four

By the time I left Elvira's, I don't know that I had achieved clarity, but I was certainly a bit tipsy. Not fully pickled, but definitely buzzed and merry. Even my right knee—which had been giving me hell—had stopped twinging, which was a good thing since I was walking home. Fortunately, it was all downhill.

My phone chimed. It was a text from Con. My heart rate kicked up a tiny bit. Okay, a lot bit.

Con: DINNER TOMORROW?

Me: SURE. WHERE?

Con: DRUNKEN PIXIE. 6pm.

He knew I hated eating late. Even before I hit thirty, I found eating too late led to indigestion. It had only gotten worse the older I got. Oh, for the cast iron stomach of a twenty-year-old. Although it did give me an excellent excuse to eat cereal for dinner.

Drunken Pixie was a marvelous Parisian themed cocktail bar that also served tasty bites. It was one of my favorite places.

Me: SOUNDS FANTASTIC. CAN'T WAIT.

Wait... Was it cool to admit I couldn't wait? Did I care if I sounded cool? Not really. That ship done sailed a long time ago.

Con: ME EITHER.

The downright giddy feeling that rushed through me was probably more appropriate for a sixteen-year-old, but I didn't care. I liked Con.

Something rustled in the bushes, and a frog streaked across the sidewalk in front of me. A frog with a paisley bowtie.

Me: GOTTA GO. FROG SITUATION.

I shoved the phone back in my pocket and took off after Kenneth.

No doubt Con thought I was crazy, but there was no time to consider that as I took off after Froggy Kenneth. The little bastard was fast, I'll give him that. He scrambled under fences, hopped over curbs, and dodged a wonky signpost on Mugwort Drive.

My breath heaved, my lungs ached, and I had developed a stitch in my side. Someone stick a sword in me. I'm done.

Froggy Kenneth clued in that I wasn't following and stopped to stare at me. His large, bulbous eyes were spooky in the dim light.

"What?" I tried to snap, but it came out more as an exhausted huff. I bent over to catch my breath. Good luck with that. "Listen, I am *trying* to turn you back into a person, or as much of one as you were before... this." I waved at his frog form. "But I can't do that if you keep running away."

"Ribbit." His tone was very reasonable. For a frog.

"Okay, then. Just come with me, and we'll go to Elvira's. She can help."

"Ribbit." I swear he nodded.

I walked slowly toward him, and he sat there calmly, waiting. The minute I reached down to grab him, he was off.

I let out a string of words that would have made a sailor blush and ran after him. This was ridiculous. I was too old for this crap.

At 3rd and Moonshadow, the frog veered toward a slightly overgrown lawn. He stopped in front of an evergreen bush that needed a good trim.

"Ribbit."

"Seriously, Kenneth. This is some nonsense. Do you want to stay a frog forever?"

Kenneth deliberately turned his back on me and stared at the house that accompanied the lawn. It was cute in a slightly bedraggled way, much like the lawn. It was one of those tiny shingle-sided beach cottages meant to weather in the salt air of the Pacific without much fuss. Probably a one bed, one bath originally built for vacations only, though like most houses in Miracle Bay, it was clearly lived in year 'round. Like the yard around it, the cottage had seen better days. Several shingles were broken and in need of replacing, the roof was on the mossy side, the top step up to the porch sagged a little, and though it was dark, I could tell by the porch light the front door needed a lick of paint. It wasn't a complete dump, but more on the shabby side. Nothing a few hours of elbow grease couldn't fix.

Kenneth stared at the cottage a moment, then back at me. There was an air of expectance about him. If a frog could be expectant. I wasn't sure. Maybe I was hallucinating this whole thing.

"Ribbit." Froggy Kenneth hopped slowly onto the patchy lawn, turning to see if I was following.

I sighed. "I'm coming."

So this is what my life had come to. Following a frog around town. Why couldn't I be a crazy cat lady like normal people?

No, Enki didn't count. For one, he wasn't a real cat. For two, well, I didn't have a second thing.

The grass came up to mid-calf and swished against my jean-clad leg. Here and there, sandy earth peeked between clumps of grass. Not only did it need mowed, but whoever owned the place should probably just pull the stuff out and put in local flora. It would do better on the coast than this sad attempt at a lawn.

"Ribbit."

I nearly tripped over Kenneth. He'd stopped in a shadowy part of the yard right in front of a strangely shaped lump. I squinted, but it was hard to see in the dark. My night vision wasn't what it was. I probably needed progressives, perish the thought.

With another sigh, I pulled my phone out of my pocket again and tapped the flashlight app, nearly blinding myself in the process. Kenneth's croak was mocking, to say the least. In this instance, I didn't blame him. I deserved mocking.

I shone the light on the lump and gasped. A pair of eyes stared back at me. A very dead pair of eyes in a very dead human face.

Froggy Kenneth had just led me to a dead body.

five

I stared down at the dead guy, my mouth gaping. You'd think by now I'd be used to stumbling across dead bodies, but my brain had fuzzed over.

This is a fine kettle of fish. Enki appeared out of nowhere—literally—and strolled toward me casually.

"Holy bananas, he's dead."

Way to state the obvious. His tone was dry as dust.

"Be careful of Kenneth," I said, suddenly remembering how I'd got there in the first place.

Who?

"The frog."

What frog?

I glanced around but there was no frog in sight. "Dammit. He ran off again."

Be that as it may, we have bigger fish to fry.

"What's with all the fish analogies?"

I'm hungry. Sue me. Have you called the police? Or that boyfriend of yours? He's at least decent eye candy.

Oh, right. Dead body. This was going to be fun to explain.

I dialed the police emergency number first and reported the body, then I sent Con a text along with the address. First a frog, then a dead guy. He was going to think I was more trouble than I was worth.

He might be right.

I shook my head. No. I wasn't going to think about myself negatively. I was no longer doormat JJ. Or at least I was working at not being doormat JJ. Work in progress.

I shone my flashlight on the dead guy again. It was hard to tell, but he looked vaguely familiar. I frowned, trying to dredge up the memory of where—or if—I'd seen him before.

A light went on in one of the windows of the cottage, and then the front door swung open. A man stood silhouetted in the light. "JJ?"

I squinted. "Eoinn? What are you doing here?"

The red-headed psychic padded down the front steps in bare feet. He was dressed in striped pajama bottoms and a gray t-shirt with the words Rose Apothecary swirled on the front. "This isn't right, is it?" he muttered to himself.

"What are you doing here, Eoinn?" I repeated.

He blinked, eyes clouded with confusion. "I live here. This is my house. Isn't it?" He glanced behind him. "Yes. Yes, it's my house."

Remember that many possible futures thing? There were some seriously weird side effects. He tended to be confused about reality a lot.

"I didn't realize you lived here." I kept my voice soothing and calm. "There's... a little problem."

He blinked again, the confusion clearing. His eyes were suddenly sparkling bright and the sharpest I'd seen them. He ran his hands through his ginger hair. "You found him, didn't you." He nodded. "Yes, I knew you would this time."

I nodded at the body. "You saw this?"

"In one of my visions. Some of my visions. Yes."

"Do you know him?" The dark-haired man huddled at my feet would have been handsome if he wasn't, you know, dead. Again, that niggle of vague recognition.

"I—" Sirens pierced the air before Eoinn could finish whatever it was he was going to say. The interruption threw him back into whatever weird fugue state he'd been in. "JJ? Is that you? I saw you—"

Good gosh, this one has the memory of a goldfish. Enki shook his head, then circled the body, sniffing at everything more like a dog than a cat.

"What are you doing?" I hissed.

"I'm standing here." Eoinn's expression was beyond confused.

Welcome to my world, buddy.

"I was talking to Enki."

I've smelled this one before. Not a fan.

"Where—?"

Car doors slammed, and I turned to see Chief of Police Xena Quintero stride across the lawn. She was tall, muscular, and totally intimidating—mostly because she could snap me in half like a twig. And not just because of her impressive muscle mass. She was an elf, which meant she had plenty of magic at her disposal, too. Tiny silver rings marched up the elegant point of each ear. Her ink-black hair was done in tiny braids pulled back with a silver clip etched with elven symbols, and her rich, dark skin glowed in the warm light from the porch. She gave me the side eye, her eyes shimmering oddly silver. I wasn't sure if it was a trick of the light or if it was an elven thing, and I wasn't about to ask.

"Fancy meeting you here." Her tone was dry as the Mojave. "It's getting to be a bad habit of yours."

She wasn't wrong. This wasn't the first time we'd met over a corpse. I swallowed, reminding myself I wasn't a doormat. "Well, yes, I do admit I have a penchant for, uh, finding things."

She snorted. "One way of putting it." She knelt down and felt for the man's pulse. "Definitely dead." She glanced up at Eoinn. "You know him?"

Eoinn shook his head, then frowned. "I don't think so?"

"That's a yes or no question, Eoinn." Her voice was firm but not unkind, as if she was used to his unusual relationship with time.

He scrunched up his face and then let out a sigh. "No. Not in this timeline."

She nodded and glanced back at the corpse. "Do you know him, Ms. Jones?"

"He looks familiar," I admitted. "But I can't place him. Like maybe I've seen him around town?" I shook my head. "Sorry, I can't remember, but I'll let you know if it comes to me."

"You do that. How'd he end up dead in your yard, Eoinn?"

Eoinn shrugged. "I don't know."

"Ms. Jones? You got any ideas?" she asked.

I swallowed. Hard. "Um, no? I just... found him here."

"And how'd you manage that?" Quintero asked.

She followed a frog. Isn't that droll? Enki's tail twitched.

"Thanks for helping," I said.

Quintero lifted an eyebrow. "He's not serious."

"Unfortunately, he is," I admitted. I wasn't sure how much to tell her. "He's an enchanted frog. Or hexed, I guess?

Part of my magic lessons with Elvira. He, um, got away, and I was trying to catch him and followed him here. I tripped over the, uh, body." Literally.

She pinched the bridge of her nose and muttered something not in English. However in the universal language, it was very much along the lines of, "What am I going to do with this idiot?"

I grimaced but forged on. "When I realized the poor man was no longer with us, I phoned the police."

A black SUV screeched to a halt behind Quintero's police car. A tall, dark-haired, broad-shouldered man in a dark suit and sunglasses stepped out and strode toward us.

"And Con, I see." Quintero shook her head.

"You'd have called him anyway," I muttered.

She ignored me. Probably for the best.

Con came straight to me and gripped my shoulders, staring into my eyes—or I assumed so since he still wore his sunglasses. He usually took them off around me, but since others were nearby, he kept them on. I guess people got freaked out by wolf eyes. Frankly, I thought they were sexy.

"Are you alright, JJ?" His expression was urgent, but his hands were gentle as they squeezed me. He lifted one hand to cup my cheek gently and warm zinged through me.

"I'm fine. Him not so much." I pointed at the dead guy.

"What have we got, Chief?" Con let me go and was immediately all business.

I think that might have been the first time I ever saw Quintero amused. "Apparently your girlfriend chased a frog into Eoinn's yard and tripped over this corpse. So, basically, par for the course with her."

I started to protest that I wasn't Con's girlfriend; we'd only been on a couple dates, but Con didn't even bat an eyelash. Instead, he knelt down beside Quintero. "Got an ID?"

She shook her head. "Waiting on the techs."

Like any other place, Miracle Bay had crime scene technicians, only here they had a lot more options available to them when it came to collecting evidence.

While the chief tried to get as much information as possible out of Eoinn—good luck to her—Con pulled me toward the street. "Did you honestly follow a frog here?"

"Yes, I did. I know it sounds nuts—"

"I've heard nuttier." His slow smile did funny things to my insides. "How about you tell the truth about this frog."

So he hadn't bought my story. No surprise there. Being a wolf shifter, he could probably smell my nervousness. I'd never been a good liar. A good prevaricator maybe, although he clearly hadn't fallen for it. So I spilled the beans about Kenneth and how I'd accidentally turned him into a frog on the day of my forty-sixth birthday. How he'd followed me here somehow and how I was trying to catch him so Elvira and I could turn him back. I was starting to think I should make a video of my explanation so I could play it anytime someone wanted to know about Froggy Kenneth.

By the end of my story, Con's lips were pressed into a firm line, his expression stern. Oh, great. Nothing like putting off your new sort-of-boyfriend by admitting you'd turned your old one into a frog. Way to put a damper on things, JJ.

But then he pressed his fist against his mouth, and I realized he was trying not to laugh.

"You jerk," I whispered. "You think this is funny!"

He let out a strangled snort-laugh. "I think it's hilarious. Only you, JJ. Only you."

I straightened my shoulders. "I don't know what you mean." I went for haughty, but it came out aggrieved.

He wrapped his arms around me and pulled me against his chest, which was currently shaking with laughter. Still, it was nice and muscley and he smelled delicious, so I didn't mind. "That you have the worst luck with magic of anyone I've ever met."

I wilted a bit. "It's true. I'm the worst witch ever."

"Hey." He gave me a squeeze. "I'm proud of you. You're working your ass off to learn everything you can, and you're getting better. Plus, you're trying to do the right thing about Konrad—"

"Kenneth."

"Whatever. He's a jackass who doesn't deserve you. It'd serve him right to spend the rest of his life as a frog." His voice was a little growly. "Yet you're doing the right thing. Trying to undo what you did even though it was an accident."

"Well, it *is* the right thing to do. Although sometimes doing the right thing sucks."

"Yeah, it does." He gave me another squeeze and let me go. "So this Keith creep led you to the body totally by accident?"

"Kenneth. And yes." I frowned. "Well, I assumed he did. How could he know there was a dead guy here?"

"How indeed?"

six

The next day was Monday, which meant Emerald had the day off and I got to handle Belle's Books and Candles (and Coffee) on my own. It was also my slowest day, so I opened at 11:00 a.m. instead of 10:00 a.m. Which was a good thing, because I overslept thanks to a late night.

Probably not a surprise it had taken me hours to get to sleep. Finding dead bodies tends to wind a person pretty tight. Or maybe that's just me.

What I needed was a pick-me-up. Something sweet to wash away last night's drama.

After questioning Eoinn and sending him back inside, Quintero ran me through my story three more times. No doubt she wanted to make sure I stuck to my guns. Naturally I did since I was telling the truth. She'd finally let me go once the techs arrived with a warning not to leave town. I'd tried really hard not to roll my eyes. Pretty sure I was wildly unsuccessful.

Since the morning was overcast and drizzly, I threw a turquoise hoodie over my jeans and *Star Trek* t-shirt and set out for The Cupcake Goddess.

As I pushed my way into the shop, my nose was hit with the scents of vanilla, lavender, and lemon. I inhaled the sugary deliciousness, immediately infused with a feeling of bliss. I swear my blood pressure dropped twenty points.

Branwen appeared from the kitchen, her beachy blonde curls done up in a pink bandana to match the pink, gold, and white decor. Like me, she wore jeans and a t-shirt, but her shirt was bedazzled across her impressive bosom: GODDESS. Nothing like truth in advertising.

"Oh, it's you," she huffed.

"Gee, good to see you, too." I might have been a little snarky.

She rolled her eyes. "Mortals. So touchy. What do you want?"

"Cupcakes."

"Duh. What kind?"

I eyed the case. How many could I get away with without looking greedy or sending myself into a sugar coma? I could always put some in the freezer. Or take a couple to my new neighbor as a welcome and sorry about staring at your naked boobs. Hallmark should totally make a card for that. "Two each chocolate, lemon lavender, and white chocolate mocha."

She took out a pink box and filled it with the requested cupcakes. Not even a hint of judgment. Granted it was her business, so it didn't pay to be judgy about a person's cupcake consumption, but she sure was judgy about darn near everything else. I suppose, being a goddess, she couldn't help herself. "Hear about the dead guy?"

I didn't bother to ask how she'd heard already. Branwen had her ways. "I found him."

She paused, tongs hovering over a purple frosted cupcake. "I'd like to say I'm surprised, but—"

"Yeah, I know." I was starting to get a reputation.

She narrowed her eyes. "You tell me all the juicy details, and I'll give you one of these for free." She waggled a cupcake at me.

"Give me two free, and it's a deal."

She grimaced. "Fine."

Once I'd paid, I gave her a quick rundown on my late-night discovery. She didn't even bat an eyelash about the frog. I wasn't sure whether that meant she was used to the weirdness of Miracle Bay, or she was getting used to my particular brand of weird. Or maybe she'd just met a lot of guys who'd been turned into frogs. It was hard to say.

"Wait, so you found the dead guy on Eoinn's lawn?" she asked as she grabbed a cupcake from the case. She swiped pink sparkly frosting off the top of the cupcake and popped it into her mouth and gave a blissful sigh. "I don't like to brag, but I make a damn fine cupcake."

She one hundred percent liked to brag. "Yep. I found the dead guy on Eoinn's lawn."

"Why?"

I frowned. "Why what?"

"Why was he in Eoinn's yard?"

"No idea," I admitted, opening my pink box and pulling out my own cupcake.

"Well, did Eoinn know him?" she pressed.

"He said not. Or rather that he didn't in this timeline. You know how he is."

She grimaced and ate another swipe of frosting. "I do. Pain in my backside. He once told me there was a timeline in which I didn't lose my powers. Fat lot of good that does me."

The thing I'd discovered about gods and goddesses was that a) they were real and b) their powers waned as their followers' beliefs did. The more attention, the more power. Which was why Thor and Loki were having a magical hey day while poor Branwen labored in near obscurity, barely able to add a hint of magic to her baked goods. She'd used nearly all her remaining power to create Miracle Bay, and she'd still needed the help of a witch to do it. A witch who happened to be my ancestor.

"Probably just a coincidence, me finding the body in Eoinn's yard. Mandrake Street is pretty dark. Not a lot of streetlights. The dead guy probably had no idea whose yard he was in. When he was alive, I mean. I sure didn't. Of course, I didn't know until last night where Eoinn lived." I took a bite of cupcake and marveled at her ability to mix chocolate and coffee in perfectly delightful proportions.

"How'd he die?"

"Not sure. I couldn't tell in the dark, even with the flashlight on my phone."

"No blood?" She picked up a piping bag and swirled more frosting on top of her now naked cupcake.

"None that I could see, but like I said, it was dark. I tried not to touch him other than to check for a pulse."

"So you don't know if it was murder, then."

I froze, cupcake halfway to my mouth for another bite. "You think he *was* murdered? Why? Why not a heart attack or something?"

She leveled me a look. "Seriously? Please. Get real, JJ. You're the Jessica Fletcher of Miracle Bay. How could it be anything else but murder?"

I wasn't sure how to take Branwen's Jessica Fletcher crack. Okay, it was true I'd stumbled across more than my

"You really should think of getting yourself one. Houseplants are wonderful friends."

She would say that. She was a plant faerie, after all. Her affinity for anything growing and green was well-known. She seemed to understand them far more than people.

I was on my way out the door when she called after me.

"JJ, don't forget to cleanse."

I blinked. I'd had a shower that morning. I gave my armpit a subtle sniff. Smelled fine. "What do you mean?"

She giggled. "Not your body. Your aura." Her expression grew grim. "So much death. You don't want it clinging to you." And then she went back to humming. It was hard to tell, but I was pretty sure it was Blue Oyster Cult's "Don't Fear the Reaper."

seven

It was just after ten, which gave me plenty of time to visit my new neighbor and hopefully get off on a better foot with cupcakes—I was down to two now—and a plant. Hopefully she wasn't a late riser, or I'd have to buy more cupcakes.

Who was I kidding? I'd be back at Branwen's tomorrow regardless.

This time, since there was no frog to chase, I went to the front door like a normal person. When Rhodore owned the place, the front porch had been clean but empty of anything except a welcome mat. After all, it had been his place of business. Dahlia apparently took a different approach.

There was a bamboo screen set up on the east end of the porch which would neatly block the view of the neighbors on that side. The west end was left open to get a good view of the beach from the rickety decoupaged card table and two mismatched kitchen chairs painted in primary colors. I'd always thought it strange that whoever built the house hadn't angled it so that it faced the ocean instead of the street, but who knew what went through the builder's mind.

The rest of the porch overflowed with potted plants. Some hung from the hooks along the front of the porch, others perched on the railing, and still others were crammed into the corners, so many that only a narrow walkway was left between them, likely for watering purposes. Marigold would approve. I was glad I'd gone with a plant. Clearly, she took the Green Witch thing literally.

Dahlia answered the door after the second knock. She wore a hot pink silk kimono that barely covered her nether regions.

"You're clothed," I blurted.

She laughed. "The first time I opened the door in the altogether I nearly gave the mail carrier a heart attack. After that, I thought I'd better cover up… at least when answering the door."

"Good plan," I said. "I doubt anyone around here has a problem with nudity, but it is a shock when you're not expecting it."

"Fair enough." Her gaze lit on the plant and the pink box. "Are those for me?"

"Yes, a sort of welcome-to-the-neighborhood-sorry-I-stared-at-your-boobs gift."

This time she laughed so hard she snorted. "Never apologize for staring at a woman's boobs. At least not *this* woman. Would you like to come in?"

"Sure." I handed her the box and the plant.

"Ohhh! Snake plant. I love it. It'll be perfect in the dining room window. Gets tons of sun."

The dining room faced the ocean and got sun all afternoon. The bay window seat was already overflowing with cacti, aloe vera, and a bunch of other plants I didn't recognize. There was a money tree which was so large it nearly blocked the built-in hutch. Even the dining table was overflowing with plants.

"You really like your plants." Lame.

"Oh, love them. I'm very into nature and growing things. The plants on the table are all herbs. I'm going to make an herb garden out back. Flowers, too. And veggies of course. But those aren't for the soap." She flipped open the pink box and squealed. "I love cupcakes!"

"Then you should check out The Cupcake Goddess. It's just down the street. Did you say soap?"

"Oh, yes. That's what I do for a living. I make soap. And sugar scrubs, bath salts, body butters. You know, that sort of thing. All made with natural ingredients, including plants and stuff I grow myself."

I felt a tingle of foreboding. Rhodore had made stuff like that, too. Only he'd gone a little too far in his search for eternal youth in moisturizer form. "Is that why you bought this place? Because the previous owner was in the business?"

She brightened. "Yes! The shed out back really sold it. It's a perfect place to brew my potions, as my brother likes to say."

The dilapidated looking shed in the back yard was, in actuality, a state-of-the-art lab where Rhodore had experimented with his face creams. I knew that everything had been removed by the witch council: all his product, research, and equipment. Only the basics were left behind like the shelving units and the six-burner stove.

I forced a smile. "Sounds perfect."

"It really is," she enthused. "I've built up a nice little business online, but I want to take it to the next level. This place will let me do that." She gave a little twirl, cupcake in each hand. "I can't wait!"

"Ribbit."

I froze. The sound came from the bay window behind me.

A huge smile crossed Dahlia's face. "Oh, *there* you are!" She shoved her cupcakes on the already crowded table and rushed over, making stupid little baby cooing noises.

I turned very slowly to find her nuzzling the ugliest frog I'd ever seen. A frog wearing a bow tie.

It gave me a baleful stare and let out a snide, "Ribbit."

"Wh-what—?" My voice sounded strangled even to my ears. "What on earth is that?"

"This is Winston. Isn't he cute?" She all but shoved him in my face. "He's my familiar."

"I'm telling you, that frog she's calling Winston is Kenneth." I paced wildly across the front room of the bookstore. Fortunately, there were currently no customers.

"You're sure?" Emerald asked from one of the armchairs next to the window. She was curled up comfortably with a freshly brewed mocha.

I gave her a look. "How many frogs wearing bow ties do you know in town?"

"Good point," she admitted.

I had called her as soon as I'd gotten back to the shop. I'd have preferred to head over to the Drunken Pixie, but it was far too early, and I'd needed to open the business. Fortunately, Emerald had been up and willing to hang out on her day off. She'd brought along Elvira who was in between yoga classes.

"And you're sure she said this frog was her familiar?" Elvira asked. She was sitting in the other armchair nursing a well-doctored Irish coffee. She didn't care if it wasn't even noon yet.

"Absolutely," I assured her. "Why do you ask?"

Elvira frowned. "Because familiars are exceedingly rare. So rare that the likelihood of two witches in a town this small both having familiars are... astronomical."

"Why are they so rare?" I asked, propping my elbows on the counter next to the register. "Con mentioned something about how all witches used to have familiars, but they didn't anymore. He didn't know why."

"Because they were hunted nearly to extinction," Elvira said grimly.

I stared at her. "What?"

"It was part of the witch trials, wasn't it?" Emerald asked. "I feel like I heard something about that." She tucked one foot under her butt.

Elvira shook her head. "That's the lie, but it was worse. Far worse."

Emerald and I exchanged glances.

"What could be worse?" I asked.

Elvira set her coffee on the end table and laced her fingers together. "It's true that many familiars were hunted down and killed along with their witches during the trials. But like witches, there were still plenty of familiars left. In fact, the vast majority of people killed, particularly the women, were innocent victims and hadn't an ounce of magic. Those that did escaped their fate."

I nodded. That made sense, actually. If a person had magic, it would be easy enough to escape mundane humans.

"It was during the trials that a particular witch grew careless and found herself on the run. She was elderly, though, and knew she would never be able to outlast her pursuers, so she cast a spell, a forbidden spell with dark purpose. She sucked the life and soul out of her familiar and used it to enhance her own strength and magic."

Emerald gasped. "That's horrific."

Elvira nodded. "It was the ultimate betrayal. The bond between familiar and witch is a sacred trust. To break it is beyond vile."

Tell that to Enki. There was nothing sacred about the way he swanned around, insulting me every chance he got. Still, I would never dream of killing him for my own gain. Or for any reason.

"She was able to escape the witch hunters quite easily after that." Elvira continued with the story. "When she realized what she'd gained by taking the life source of a familiar, she decided to do it again. So she tricked her sister's familiar and murdered him as well. This time, the energy shaved years off, making her decades younger. Her magic grew stronger. But it wasn't enough."

"Let me guess. She hunted down every familiar she could get her hands on." It wasn't a difficult leap to make.

"She did. And there were unscrupulous others who discovered her secret and went on the hunt, too. Soon the numbers of familiars had dwindled so much that it was feared they would be lost forever. That is when the first witch council was formed. It took all their collective power to stop the witches and protect the few remaining familiars."

Emerald shook her head. "That's horrible. What happened to the ones who were left?"

"Those who wished to stay with their witches did so. Those who did not were allowed passage into Elfame. What humans call Fairyland. Familiars can pass easily between the two realms." She shook her head. "They've regained much of their numbers since, but most refuse to return to our world to companion witches."

"Can't say I blame them," I said dryly. "I assume Enki was so unpleasant they threw him out."

Both Emerald and Elvira laughed.

"Enki is the familiar of your family line," Elvira said. "Has been for centuries. Which might explain his attitude." She winked. "Although he seems to spend a lot more time in our realm since you arrived."

"Why did I luck out?" I asked.

"I'm not sure," Elvira admitted. "Might be to do with your particular brand of magic."

Which we still hadn't figured out yet. "Yay me. But what about Dahlia?"

"What about her?" Elvira asked.

"If familiars are as rare as you say, why does she think she has one?"

Emerald smirked. "And that it's Froggy Kenneth."

"That's an interesting question," Elvira mused. "It had to have been a recent development since Kenneth has only been a frog a short time."

"And she should know he's not a familiar," Emerald pointed out. "A witch can spot a familiar a mile away."

It was true. Everyone in town knew Enki was a familiar before I did. To me, he was just annoying. Well, sometimes he was marginally helpful. "Could she truly believe Froggy Kenneth is her familiar?"

Elvira snorted. "If she does, she's dumb as a box of rocks."

"Could be under a spell," Emerald suggested. "Maybe somebody put a hex on Dahlia so she'd think he was her familiar."

Something occurred to me. Something very much darker. "Or worse. They're in cahoots."

eight

By the end of the night, we still hadn't come up with a good way to uncover the truth about Dahlia and Froggy Kenneth. Elvira had even tried to use her librarian superpowers to research Dahlia's past, but she hadn't come up with much other than what we already knew. She had lived her entire life in a magical commune somewhere back east. It wasn't until she bought the house here in Miracle Bay that her name was on any other records anywhere in the country.

Unfortunately, Con had to cancel our date, what with dead guys popping up on lawns, so I went to bed early. I was half asleep when I got a text from Maude—one of the vampire Golden Girls—asking if I'd come to tea the next evening. Since offending vampires was a bad idea and I didn't have other plans, I sent her a text back telling her I'd be there. I'd no idea what vampires served for tea, but their cookies were darn tasty.

The day flew by in a whirlwind. Lots of people needed books, and I had several online orders for my specialty books to pack and ship.

Agnes had started an online shop selling the more valuable esoteric books she came across. Some were valuable simply because they were rare, old editions that were highly collectable. Some had belonged to famous supernaturals and so were desirable much like Jane Austen's diary would be. Yet others were truly magical, holding spells and incantations of great power. It was this part of the business that made the real money. I was also finding it to be the most interesting and terrifying as it required a lot of research and consideration on my part. The books had to be inspected to ensure nothing truly dangerous got out into the world. My grandmother had acquired and vetted most of the current stock, but I would soon need to start doing that side of things myself. It would help if I could get a handle on my magic before that happened.

Emerald was busy with readings all day, so we barely had time to talk, and when I texted Elvira to see if she'd discovered anything, her response was a brusk, "Chill."

I'd never thought I'd have an eighty plus woman telling me to chill.

I wasn't sure what a person wore to tea with vampires, so after work I dressed in a simple green knee-length wrap dress with three-quarter sleeves and a pair of black ballet flats. It was nice enough for a night out, but not so fancy as to be out of place anywhere. Since I was out of plants and cupcakes, I selected a book of poetry as a hostess gift. I didn't know about the others, but Maude was a romantic, so I figured she'd like it at least, and the invite had come from her.

Enki joined me on the vampires' porch.

"What are you doing here?" I smacked the doorknocker shaped like a banana. No, I don't mean the fruit kind.

I was invited, he said in an exasperated tone. *What do you think?*

"And exactly how did they manage that? You don't have a phone."

He gave me a smug look. *I have my ways.*

The door swung open revealing Maude in all of her frilly glory. She looked to be around seventy with fluffy silver hair that sprung wildly from her head, bright blue eyes, and a vague smile. She wore a ruffled butter yellow apron and under that a neatly pressed navy-blue shirtwaist dress that emphasized her resplendent curves.

"Come in! Come in!" She stepped back to let us enter. "We're just so glad you're here. You'd be surprised, but we don't have that many visitors."

I wasn't that surprised, actually. Everyone loved the four vampires they referred to as Miracle Bay's Golden Girls, but there was still something nerve wracking about dining with a vampire. Or four.

Maude led me not back to the kitchen where I'd hung out with the Golden Girls before, but to the formal dining room. Like the rest of the house, it was done in overly floral style, ala Laura Ashley at the height of '80s fashion, though the color scheme here was an unusual celery green. Seemed an odd choice for a dining room, but nobody asked me.

The table had been laid with a gorgeous Royal Albert Lavender and Rose tea set along with tea tiers made from mismatched antique china. There was a vintage record player in the corner playing old jazz from the '20s. The scent of baked goods made my stomach rumble. And, much to my surprise, there was an unexpected guest.

"Eoinn?"

"JJ!" He jumped up and nearly knocked me over with a giant hug.

Once I'd gotten my breath back, I took the seat Maude indicated and spread my cloth napkin on my lap. I looked up to find five pairs of eyes staring at me expectantly. Well, six, if you counted Enki, which I didn't since he was face first in a scone covered in clotted cream and jam.

"What?" I asked. My tone was defensive, but my gut fluttered nervously.

"Don't be a ninny. We aren't going to eat you." Harriet grinned. Like Maude, she appeared in her early seventies with silver white hair cut in a short shag. She was handsome rather than beautiful, and her well-cut beige pantsuit showed off her tall, broad-shouldered figure extremely well.

"You wish," muttered Daphne in her slight Southern accent. "I don't think you're her type, honey."

"Don't be an idiot, Daphne." Harriet scowled at the other vampire.

"Kids these days." Stella shook her head. "No backbone."

I had no idea if she was referring to me or the bickering vampires.

"Stop it you three. You're worrying the poor girl for nothing," Maude chided. "Tea, JJ, dear? It's Paris from Harney and Sons. It's really delicious."

"Yes, please." I wasn't much of a tea drinker, but Paris tea was my favorite. The rich black tea was flavored with fruit, caramel, and vanilla. With a little cream and sugar added, it was heaven in a cup.

As Maude poured my drink, I slathered my scone with cream and jam and plucked a pink macaron from one of the tiers. "Maybe you better tell me why I'm here, then, since it's obviously not about tea."

"It *is* about tea, dear," Maude insisted. "It's such a vital part of life, don't you think? Why we used to have tea every Saturday back on the farm—"

"Shut it, Maude. You're getting off topic." Harriet turned to me. "Our poor resident psychic here has managed to get himself arrested."

"What?!" I turned to Eoinn, eyes wide. "Is that true?"

"Not exactly." He blushed, poking at his scone with his butter knife. "I'm a 'person of interest,' according to the chief."

"Trust me, you are a breath away from ending up in the pokey." Stella stabbed her fork in his general direction.

"Don't exaggerate," Harriet said.

"Who's exaggerating? They've practically got him tied up for murder. In my day, they'd have hung him by now."

My eyes grew wider. "Murder? I think somebody had better explain."

Why the shock? You're the one who found the body, Enki said, swiping a pink tongue at a generous dollop of clotted cream.

"I know I found a body, but I didn't realize he'd been murdered," I pointed out.

"He was," Harriet confirmed. "I don't know all the details, but Lemon down at the police station called me when they brought Eoinn in for questioning."

I knew Lemon. I'd met her during a previous investigation. She'd told me that she and my grandmother had "similar interests." I still had no idea what that meant. I'd had no idea she was close to the Golden Girls.

"Why did she call you?" I asked.

"She knows I promised the boy's mother I'd look out for him." Harriet popped a macaron in her mouth and chewed with gusto.

The "boy" in question was well past forty. But I got it. Eoinn could easily get lost in the threads of his psychic visions. He needed somebody to look out for him.

"Did Lemon say how he was murdered?" I asked.

"She did not," Harriet admitted. "I tried to get it out of her, but that one is closed as a clam when she wants to be."

That was for sure.

"He was shot," Eoinn said almost dreamily.

"No, he wasn't," I said. The dead man hadn't had a scratch on him, and there wasn't a drop of blood anywhere. That much I remembered.

Eoinn frowned, his eyes nearly crossing with the effort to focus on something only he could see. "No... wait... poison... no..."

I sighed. "Basically, we don't know."

"No, we don't, honey. Maybe you could sweet talk that cutie patootie of yours into spilling the beans," Daphne suggested.

No doubt she was referring to Con. I bet he'd love being called a cutie patootie. But she did have a point. He probably knew how the guy got killed.

"Okay, forget method of murder for the moment. Why do the police think you did it?" I asked Eoinn. "You know, other than the fact the guy was found on your lawn."

"Which could have happened to anybody," Maude said, patting his hand.

He shrugged helplessly. "He was my ex?"

"You said in another timeline he was your ex," I reminded him gently. "You said in this one you never met."

"Um." He pressed his lips together. "I... It's not clear."

"Focus, Eoinn," Harriet urged. "Remember to find your center and all that."

He nodded. "Right." He closed his eyes and took a deep breath. "Yes, in another timeline he was my ex. Several other timelines, actually."

"But not every timeline?" I urged.

"No, not every timeline. And definitely not this one. We hadn't even met yet." He looked a little sad. "And now we never will."

"Do you know his name?" I asked.

A small smile teased his lips. "Gil."

"Gil what?"

He shrugged helplessly.

"Did Gil always get, ah, dead in every timeline?" I asked as delicately as I could. Not that there was a delicate way to ask about murder.

He swayed a little, his forehead wrinkling from the sustained concentration. "Yes. He always ends up murdered. It's one of those... irrefutable moments in time."

Interesting, though not helpful. "Can you see who killed him? Is it always the same?"

"I don't know if it's always the same, but I can see who the killer is in one timeline. Or at least who was convicted of the crime."

"Who?" We all spoke at once.

He opened his eyes, face pale. "Me."

nine

I don't know when I became the Jessica Fletcher of Miracle Bay, but I knew I had to help Eoinn. He was my friend. A new friend and an odd one, but a friend none-the-less.

And I didn't believe for one second he'd murdered Gil of no last name. Not in this timeline, not in any. He might have been convicted in one timeline or other, but I didn't buy it, and I wasn't going to let him be railroaded by anyone. Chief Quintero was good at her job, but it was easy to put on blinders during an investigation, and I wasn't going to let that happen to Eoinn.

Problem was, I didn't have a lot to go on. Since the Golden Girls had suggested I could get more information out of Con, I figured that was as good as any place to start, so the next morning, I sent a quick text asking when we could meet.

His response was almost immediate: NOW IS GOOD.

Crap on a cracker. I was still in bed, wearing my flamingo pajamas, my hair up in a messy bun. I hadn't even had coffee yet.

It would probably take him a few minutes to get there, though. Maybe I had time to make myself presentable.

Me: ETA?

Con: I'M OUTSIDE.

I flew out of bed. My foot got caught up in the sheet and nearly sent me sprawling. I managed to untangle myself and staggered toward the window. Sure enough, Con's black SUV was parked in the street out front of my shop.

"Frickity frack!"

Oh, this is going to be so droll. Enki appeared literally out of nowhere and hopped up to perch on my bed.

"You better not shed on my duvet," I snapped.

Or what?

"I have been known to turn people into frogs, you know."

Perish the thought. He didn't sound at all worried. Drat him.

I sent Con another text: 5 MIN.

I glanced down at the car. Con deliberately turned his face up toward me then gave me the thumbs up. My face turned pink. He knew I'd been watching. Drat the man.

I spun from the window and ran to the bathroom where I quickly brushed my teeth and hair and slapped on some extra deodorant. I rummaged through the closet, throwing clothes willy nilly, trying to find something to wear.

What's wrong with the flamingos?

"I can't let Con see me in my pajamas. He'll think I'm a weirdo."

You are *a weirdo. Let your freak flag fly.*

I stared at him. I mean, just imagine Alan Rickman telling you to let your freak flag fly. It was bizarre.

What? I'm hip.

I snorted. "Yes, very hip." I finally found a plum-colored jersey knit maxi dress, so I threw that on and added a cardigan over the top since it promised to be a cool day. Then I rushed downstairs to let Con in.

He eyed me appreciatively. "You look nice."

"Thanks." I glanced down. He wasn't wrong. The dress gave me some pretty impressive cleavage.

"The pajamas were cute, too."

My cheeks burned. "Coffee?"

"Sure. But I'd like something else first."

I stared at him blankly, then my eyes widened as he leaned in and claimed my lips with his. I completely forgot I was barefoot, standing on the front porch, freezing my butt off. His kisses were that good.

It wasn't until a passer-by wolf-whistled that we finally pulled away.

While I fired up the coffee machine in the cafe, he took a seat on one of the barstools. I swear I could feel his gaze on me. He was a predator, after all, in more ways than one.

"Let me guess. This isn't a social call." He sounded amused.

"What do you mean?"

"You texted me at eight in the morning."

"Ah." He knew I wasn't a morning person. "You're right, this isn't social. Not entirely," I admitted as I brought him a cappuccino. "Although I did want to see you."

He slid his hand over mine, his skin warmer than a human's, as he took the mug from me. "That's good. I wanted to see you, too."

I raised a brow as I took a sip of my own drink. "Is that why you were stalking my house at this ridiculous hour?"

He grinned. "Maybe I just needed a new book."

"You bought three last week."

He shrugged. "I like to read." He gave me a meaningful look. "And I like spending time with you."

I grinned. When I was in my twenties, I'd have probably played coy and pretended like being with him was no big deal, but I was too old to play games. Especially when it came to a guy like Con. "I like spending time with you, too."

"I'm sorry I had to cancel."

"It's okay. You had a good reason."

"Unfortunately." He eyed me over the rim of his mug. "Let me guess. You want to know more about our victim and how he died."

"You know me too well." I poured an extra spoonful of raw sugar into my cappuccino. "I'm just curious."

He gave me a look that told me I hadn't fooled him one bit. "It's a weird one. I'll give you that."

"Weird how?" Other than a frog leading me to a dead body.

"First off, the victim, Gilmore Benedict—according to his identification—wasn't from around here."

"Gilmore?" I gaped. "What kind of name is that?"

"It's an old witch bloodline. One that's extinct. The Gilmores were powerful, but the last one died a hundred years ago, although there are plenty of non-magical humans who bear the name. My guess is someone had hopes for their son."

"Despite witch magic being only passed to women?"

He shrugged. "Who knows? Rumor has it some of the old bloodlines did have male practitioners. It's hard to say."

"Was this Gil magical?"

"Well, he definitely wasn't a witch."

My eyes narrowed. "That doesn't answer the question."

"Quintero and her people detected no magic in him," Con admitted. "Neither did I."

"How is that possible? Only magical people can enter Miracle Bay." My thoughts flew to Froggy Kenneth. There had to be a connection there.

"Only magical people can enter without help. A non-magical person can enter as long as they're with someone magical or they have the right talisman, as you know."

I did know. I'd nearly been murdered because of it.

"Okay, so he's likely non-magical which means somebody let him in." Just like Froggy Kenneth. "How and why did he end up dead on Eoinn's front lawn?"

"Why, I don't know, but as to how..." Con shook his head. "We're waiting on the autopsy for that, but it's clear nobody except Eoinn recognized him."

"Eoinn only recognized him from visions," I pointed out. I thought about mentioning that Gilmore Benedict had looked familiar to me, but since I still couldn't place him, I figured it was pointless. He probably reminded me of someone on TV or something.

"So he says."

"You don't believe him?"

Con sighed and shoved a lock of hair out of his face. It fell right back down like a Superman curl. It was adorable, but I wasn't about to tell him that. "Eoinn doesn't always know what's real and what isn't. Sometimes he gets confused between what he sees in his visions and what's really happened."

"So you think he could have met this Gil person—only mixed it up with his visions?"

"Or he's lying."

I glared at him. "Seriously? Do you kick puppies, too?"

He rolled his eyes. "You're adorable when you're outraged. No, I don't truly think Eoinn is involved, but so far, the evidence points to him. We have to go where the evidence leads."

"What evidence?"

He shifted as if suddenly uncomfortable, which was unusual to say the least. "Our medical examiner is a medium. She can catch glimmers of a soul's final moments. She says Gilmore Benedict was hexed to death."

"Hexed to death? That's a thing?" I knew hexes were a thing. I even knew a couple though I'd never used them. But killing someone with one? That was new.

He nodded. "It can be done, but it takes a powerful magic practitioner."

"You mean witch." As far as I knew, only witches could cast hexes. Enchantments could be cast by just about anyone with magic, but you needed a witch to hex someone.

"Yes. Probably. Although a non-witch could have hired a witch to cast the hex."

There was an interesting idea. Could someone in Miracle Bay have cast a hex strong enough to kill a man? For money? I'd have to check with Elvira to see if anyone was strong enough to do that. She probably could, but I knew she'd never do such a thing.

"So why does Quintero think Eoinn did it? What evidence is there other than that the victim was found in his yard?" That wasn't damning enough, as far as I was concerned.

"Eoinn could have cast the hex."

I stared at him. "That's impossible. Eoinn is a psychic, not a witch." The most he could have done was hire a witch to cast a hex, and I couldn't imagine he'd do that.

"Eoinn is a psychic, true, but his magic comes from the varo-lokkur."

I shook my head. "Never heard of the varo-lokkur."

"It's an ancient line of male magical practitioners. Loosely translated it means 'caller of spirits.'"

"I don't see what that has to do with anything."

"A varo-lokkur is the only being other than a witch who has the power to cast a hex."

ten

I stared at Con for a long beat. "Seriously?"

"Seriously. While I've never known him to do it, Eoinn is capable of casting a hex."

I downed the last of my coffee. "Nope. Don't buy it."

His eyebrows raised over ice blue eyes. He rarely went without his sunglasses—his wolf eyes freaked people out—but he had started taking them off around me. "What do you mean?"

"For one, I don't believe for a second that Eoinn would hex anyone. For another, if that's all Quintero has to go on, that's flimsy as heck. I'm capable of casting a hex, and I'm the one who found the body. Is she going to arrest me now?"

"Are you volunteering?"

I snorted. "Hardly." Granted it was probably dumb to admit I was as good a suspect as Eoinn, but here we were. "Point is, there are plenty of people in this town who could have hexed that man."

"And yet none of them dated him."

"Not even Eoinn," I pointed out. At least not in this timeline. "Even if he did, that's hardly a reason to murder someone."

"You turned your ex into a frog," Con pointed out.

"Oh, low blow!"

He smirked. "I couldn't help myself. You just left it lying there."

"And you had to pick it up." I shook my head, amused.

"Of course I did. You wouldn't have respected me if I didn't."

He had a point. "Back to the subject at hand. We need to know more about this Gilmore Benedict person."

"We?" His lips twitched again.

"Of course, we. You're my inside man."

"I don't think the council would consider helping you part of my job."

"What the council doesn't know won't hurt me."

"Elvira is on the council," he pointed out.

"And?"

"She knows you're investigating, right? She'll know you've roped me in."

"Won't be the first time." I wasn't worried about it. Elvira was my step-grandmother. It gave me a lot of leeway. Well, sometimes.

"Fine." He caved a little too easily. "How do you propose we go about investigating our victim?"

"I figured I'd start with the great oracle, Google," I said. "Although that will be limited to things mundane. If he was involved with the magical community in any way, I doubt I'll be able to find that out."

"I can handle that part," he offered. "I've got access to information you don't have."

"Okay, it's a plan. Can you send me his photo?"

"Sure, but why?"

"Figured I could show it around, ask if anyone recognizes him."

He climbed off his stool. "Good idea. I'll send it over later. I'm off. I'll meet you at the Drunken Pixie at seven."

I blinked. "What?"

"For dinner. You eat, right?"

"Of course I do. You know I do. But you didn't exactly ask me out properly."

He smirked. "We're comparing notes."

"Oh." Well, damn.

My face must have shown my disappointment because he circled the counter, wrapped one arm around me, and pulled me against him.

"Don't sound so upset. Dinner first—because I know you need regular feeding—and we'll compare notes."

He wasn't wrong about regular feeding. I got cranky if I didn't eat. "And after we compare notes?"

"After that... the night is ours." He leaned down and pressed his lips to mine.

Seriously, you two. Get a room. Enki strolled in and hopped up on the stool Con had just vacated. *How about some coffee for me? I've had a rough night.*

I pulled away from Con, rolling my eyes. "Yes, your majesty."

"I'll see you tonight." Con pressed a quick kiss to my forehead.

"Let me walk you to the door."

After another, lengthier kiss, I finally let Con go. I watched his car disappear down the road then turned to go back inside. Branwen's gold statue caught my eye, and I stared at it. Something niggled at the back of my head. A vague memory…

That's why Gilmore Benedict looked familiar. He'd been in my shop, asking about the statue on the day he died. I should probably tell Quintero, not that it would help anything. I couldn't see what the dead guy poking around a statue had to do with anything.

I stepped back inside and closed the door behind me but left it unlocked and flipped the sign. It was early still, but since I was up, I might as well be open.

Ugh. The two of you make my teeth hurt, Enki said as I reentered the café.

"You're just jealous," I said as I whipped him up his own cappuccino, extra foam. It seemed like a weird thing to give a cat, but as Enki often reminded me, he only looked like a cat.

As if. Now hurry up with my drink.

"Can I ask you a question?" I asked as the espresso dripped its slow way from the machine into a mug.

Enki eyeballed me suspiciously. *Depends.*

"Why are you still a familiar?"

What do you mean? He sounded far too innocent.

"I mean, there are so few of you left and most fled to the fae realm. Why stay here?"

Seemed like the thing to do at the time. Now are you going to bring me my drink? I'm dying of thirst here.

I dumped the espresso into a bowl and added hot milk and foam. "But why did you choose my family? Why me?"

Why not? He eyed the bowl in my hands. *Although I'm starting to wonder why myself.*

It was clear he wasn't in the mood to answer my questions. Which was pretty much par for the course with him.

After I placed his majesty's cappuccino bowl on the counter where he could reach it, I padded to the front and began unboxing a new shipment of books. There was a thump on the front steps, and I glanced outside. Eugene Bramble—one of Emerald's regulars—made his painstaking way up to the porch, so I opened the door for him.

He shuffled inside, pure white hair fluffed up wildly like a dandelion. He was slender, boob-high on me, and had a wide, friendly smile and thick glasses. He probably should use a cane but refused to. Said it made him feel old. I got that.

"Emerald isn't in yet, Eugene."

He offered me a bemused smile. "I'm early. I could really go for a latte, JJ. Something with a kick."

"You know I don't have a liquor license." Not to mention it wasn't even noon yet.

He gave me a look. "Ain't nobody needs to know but you, me, and that cat of yours."

Not a cat. Enki was whiskers deep in his coffee. *But I wouldn't mind an extra kick.*

"I don't want to get shut down for serving alcohol without a license."

Eugene snorted. "Who's going to bother?"

"The council?"

"They got better things to do with their time. Besides, if you serve me a coffee, and I happen to add a little something while your back is turned, who's to know?"

"I guess you have a point." I repressed a smile.

He grinned. "'Course I do. You'll have to provide the something, though."

"Of course I do."

"Don't worry." He shot me a wink. "I'll make it worth your time."

I sighed. "Give me a minute."

It didn't take long for me to whip up a mug of rich, black coffee. I added in half and half, sugar, cinnamon, nutmeg, and just a hint of ginger. I gave it a good stir, imbuing the brew with vitality. Then I pulled a plain brown bottle from the cupboard and passed both it and the drink to Eugene.

He unscrewed the bottle and gave it a sniff. "Chocolate liquor. That's a start."

I rolled my eyes and got down a bottle of whiskey.

"That's more like it." He added heavy dollops of the booze to both his drink and Enki's.

Much obliged.

I put the bottles away and then carried Eugene's drink to the comfortable armchairs in the window. It was a gloomy day, and the ocean boiled gray and angry. A little rain spit against the window.

Once he was seated, drink in hand, Eugene gave me an enigmatic smile. "I hear you've been investigating our latest little murder."

"Little murder" was an interesting way to put it. "How'd you hear that?" I asked as I went back to unpacking the new books.

He tapped the side of his nose. "I have my ways."

"If you must know, yes. I'm trying to figure out who he is, who killed him, and why."

"I take it you don't think Eoinn is involved." He took a sip of coffee and let out a blissful sigh. "Nirvana. And I don't mean that weird band from the '90s."

I bit my tongue about the "weird" comment. Not that I was a big Nirvana fan, but he was one to talk about weird. "No, I don't think Eoinn had anything to do with it."

"Nor do I. So we are in agreement."

Strange bedfellows. "I guess so. But why do you care?"

"Eoinn's my nephew. Didn't I say?"

"Er, no." I tried to picture the diminutive, wizened Eugene being related to the tall, lanky Eoinn and got nothing. The two looked nothing alike.

"My sister's kid. Well, half-sister. She was quite a bit younger than me. But blood is blood, and magic is magic."

I had no idea what that meant, but I nodded. "Indeed."

"Well, now, this follow. Gil Whatsis."

"Yes, Gilmore Benedict."

"What a name." He took another hefty swallow. "That's the ticket." He smacked his lips with enthusiasm. "I saw him you know."

"Eoinn?" I was a little confused about where this was heading.

"Naw, the other guy. What'd you call him? Galahad?"

"Gilmore."

"Yeah, him."

I leaned forward eagerly. "Where'd you see him? Here in town?"

"Of course here in town. I haven't left Miracle Bay in a decade. Don't see a point in it."

"When did you see him?" I pressed.

His eyebrows scrunched into one long, beetley brow as if he was doing math sums in his head. "Couple days ago."

I stiffened. That was the same day Froggy Kenneth had shown up on my porch. It couldn't be a coincidence, could it? "What was he doing? When you saw him? Was he with anyone?"

"Several someones, actually." He drained his coffee, set the mug on the side table, and wandered over to the shelf that held the new releases. "Anything interesting in the way of thrillers?"

"Sure." I grabbed a couple and handed them to him. "Who were the someones?"

He squinted. "Eh?"

"That Gil was talking to when you saw him?"

"Oh, right." His eyes twinkled. "It was those skyclad dancers."

"The what now?" Naturally, I'd heard of skyclad—Dahlia had just mentioned it—but he made it sound like a girl gang.

"Bunch of women. They get together on full moons and whatnot, dance naked around campfires and cast spells. You know the thing." He scanned the back of one of the thrillers. His eyes lit up. "This one sounds good."

"Great." I took it from him. "I'll ring it up. So... skyclad... like witches?"

"Mostly. Though there are some others."

"Like who?"

"No idea. It's kinda hush-hush."

"Not that hush-hush if you know about it," I pointed out.

He chuckled. "True. But then I'm nosier than most."

"But you said Gil was talking to some of them. Who was he talking to specifically?"

"Lemon, for one."

"The receptionist at the police station?" She hadn't struck me as the sort to go skyclad.

"That's the one."

"Wow. You never know about people, do you?"

"No, you do not."

"And the rest?"

"Abilene Simpson. She's been a member of the group since she got her first spark of magic. Oh, and Molly Tipanny. I think she goes more for the cake than anything else."

"How'd you know it was anything to do with the skyclad thing? It could have been coincidence."

"Doubtful. Lemon doesn't much care for people. For her, it's work and the group, and the rest of the time, she locks herself away in her castle."

"Metaphorically."

He gave me a look. "No. Why would it be metaphorical?"

Why indeed. "Okay, so this random stranger was talking to women from this skyclad group and then turns up dead a couple days later." I didn't mention that in between he'd shown up in my shop, asking strange questions and then inspecting a statue. "You don't think that's odd?"

He shrugged. "This is Miracle Bay. I see at least six odd things before breakfast."

He had a point.

"I'm surprised you didn't know about the skyclad dancers," he said.

"What do you mean?"

"Your grandmother, Agnes, was a member."

I nearly choked on my tongue.

eleven

I found it difficult to wrap my head around the idea of Agnes Jones dancing naked in the moonlight with a bunch of other women. Elvira, sure, I could see it. But Agnes? She hadn't seemed the type.

Then again, what did I really know about my grandmother other than that her ghost was bossy as heck? I hadn't seen her in a while, but Elvira assured me she was still around.

What I did know was that the best way, other than Google, to find out more information on Gilmore Benedict—particularly why he was in town—was to have a chat with Lemon. She'd helped me before. Maybe she would again.

I quickly dialed the police station, expecting Lemon to pick up, only to get one of the deputies. His voice was muffled as if his mouth was half full. "Miracle Bay Police. This is Deputy Tran."

"Hi, this is JJ Jones. Is Lemon available?"

"Nope." Chewing sounds filtered down the line.

"Do you know when she will be?"

"Nope." More chewing sounds.

Flames... on the side my face... flaming...

"Do you know how I can reach her?"

"Probably have to walk."

Huh? "What now?"

"Well, you can't drive out there."

I gritted my teeth. "Drive out where?"

"The promontory, 'course. That's where they do their rituals."

I pinched the bridge of my nose. "Who do?"

Deputy Tran lowered his voice. "The skyclad dancers. You know. Chief don't like it much."

"I thought it was all live and let live around here." Barring a few murders, of course.

"It is. But Lemon always takes along her magical moonshine and things get a little... excitable."

Oh, boy. "And everyone in town knows about this?" Except me, apparently.

"Pretty much. Surprised you don't. Your grandmother started it."

"Started it? I have so many questions."

"I'd ask Lemon. She knows where all the bodies are buried. Not literally." There was a thoughtful pause with more chewing. "I don't think."

Oh, goodie. "Can you tell me how to get to this promontory?"

"Sure thing." He gave me pretty decent directions I hoped I could follow. GPS could be dodgy in Miracle Bay. "But they won't be out there until after dark."

Which meant after eight. Good thing, since dinner with Con was at seven. "How long do they stay out, do you know?"

"No idea. At least midnight or so. I only know because last year, I had to arrest a couple of them for drunk and disorderly."

"Thanks, Deputy. I appreciate your help."

"Sure thing, Ms. Jones."

After I hung up, I tucked the directions into my purse. It was still an hour until closing and two hours until dinner with Con, so I spent the time on my phone, searching for any sign of the victim online. That netted me a big fat zero. Nobody named Gilmore Benedict existed anywhere that I could find. Not on social media, not even on those statistics sites. I even checked Ancestry to no avail.

Con had emailed me a picture of Gilmore Benedict. Unfortunately, it was pretty clear he was dead, which would probably creep people out. Fortunately, there were plenty of photo manipulation apps to help with that. A few tweaks, and he looked much more alive, complete with open eyes and a healthy flush to his skin. It would certainly be enough to show people without freaking them out. I printed out a copy and stuck it in my purse with the directions.

Finally, I flipped the closed sign and headed upstairs to get changed. I wouldn't normally drive to the Drunken Pixie, but since I planned to head out to the promontory after, I took my car.

The Drunken Pixie looked like any other bar anywhere in the country. The shingle siding was silvery gray with age, a chalkboard with the day's cocktail hung next to the double doors, and a simple blue awning, slightly faded, hung over the front to protect patrons from the spitting rain.

Inside was another matter. It had been decorated like a Parisian salon from the wide-planked floors to the Belle Epoque chandeliers, French Regency frames on the walls to the Louis XV style furniture. Even the music playing over the sound system was French.

Con waited for me in one of the plush velvet booths. He even had a cocktail waiting, along with slices of baguette and baked brie and figs. He knew me well.

I gave him a peck then slid into the booth and picked up my cocktail. "Only one. I've got some sleuthing to do."

His brow rose. "Sleuthing?"

"I found nothing about Gilmore Benedict online. He either doesn't exist, or he's been living off the grid his whole life." I took a sip of bright, sweet, violet and gin. "Mmm… Aviation. Perfection."

He raised his own glass. Old Fashioned. "I know how you like them."

"I do. Now, what'd you find on Gil?" I grabbed a piece of bread, slathered it with gooey cheese, and popped it in my mouth. Heaven.

"Like you, nothing. There is no Gilmore Benedict in any database, magical or otherwise."

I sat down my drink. "How is that possible?"

He shrugged. "I don't know. My best guess is that his ID was fake, and Gilmore Benedict is not his real name."

"What about his DNA, fingerprints, a reverse photo search?"

He shook his head. "Nothing."

I frowned. "Something is hinky."

"Agreed. Unfortunately, I'm not sure what that is."

"Which leads me to my sleuthing." I took a sip of my cocktail. Delish. "I'm going to go see Lemon tonight. Apparently, she spoke to Gil before he died. Word on the street is if anyone knows anything, she does."

"Word on the street?" he teased.

"You know what I mean."

He reached over and tangled his fingers with mine. "I do. Now how about we forget about murder and talk about something more… interesting."

"More interesting than murder?" I teased back. "I'll do my best, but I'm not sure I can top that."

After dinner, I was reluctant to leave for my sleuthing rendezvous. In fact, I probably would have cancelled, but Con got a call from Quintero and had to go, so it was back to the original plan for me.

Tran had assured me there was parking up on the promontory, but that I'd have to walk out to the end where Lemon and her group held their skyclad magical moonshine-infused shenanigans. The deputy's words, not mine. Though I did like the sound of it.

Naturally tonight was a full moon. And not just any full moon—a Pink Moon. According to Elvira, it signified rebirth and renewal. It was also a good time to focus on romantic relationships. She'd winked at me when she said it. Guess it was a good thing Con and I had our date that night. Although I hadn't realized at the time it was the Pink Moon.

I was the worst witch ever.

Then again, I suppose there was more to witchcraft than knowing all the full moons and their meanings. After all, I hadn't been raised a witch. I was still trying to catch up.

I took the road leading out of town to the south. Well, technically it didn't actually leave town. It meandered up the side of the promontory, giving drivers teasing glimpses of the town and the ocean between thick stands of Sitka spruce before ending at a footpath out to the very end of the promontory overlooking the ocean.

The parking lot was almost full when I got there. Several cars were parked haphazardly as if their drivers had been too eager to get on with the party to pull inside the lines properly. Not that there were actual lines painted in the hard packed dirt and gravel, but you get what I mean.

As I climbed out of the car, my nose tingled with woodsmoke layered over salt air. The lot was lit only by moonlight, and I had to use my flashlight app to pick my way toward the footpath. Once I hit it, though, lights sprung to life, outlining the narrow path between the trees. They were unusual, though, the lights, swaying slightly in the breeze off the ocean. I leaned down to get a better look and realized that they were made of old glass floats, which explained the rainbow of colors. Thin cords had been knotted around them, then looped over iron hooks screwed into driftwood posts spaced haphazardly along the path. Inside each float was a small creature that glowed brighter than a dozen lightening bugs and looked like a demon pixie with razor sharp teeth and hostile red eyes. One charged at the glass as if it wanted to chomp on my nose.

I flinched away. I'd have been embarrassed by my reaction, but I figured it was natural. Those things were creepy.

I continued down the path, the lights dimming behind me. It was clever, but maybe not... awesome. Keeping living creatures trapped in glass like that didn't feel right, even if they were scary. The idea of confronting Lemon, of all people, about it made me even more uncomfortable, but I was definitely going to do it. How could I not? I may be a recovering doormat, but I knew it was the right thing to do.

The path wound around enormous clusters of ferns, rhododendrons, and pine trees, finally ending in a wide-open space at the tip of the promontory. A bonfire blazed in the middle of the clearing while half a dozen women danced around it. A boombox straight out of the '80s pumped out an instrumental piece that I was almost one hundred percent sure was a New Age version of "Get Low." I swear I had a vision of Betty White in that movie, dancing around the fire and singing along to the East Side Boyz.

Sure enough, my nudist neighbor was at the head of the pack, her blonde hair streaming wildly in the wind and her impressive bosoms bouncing around like bowling balls in the backseat of a getaway car. My back hurt just thinking about it.

I didn't recognize the other women—likely some of the ones Eugene had mentioned—except for one: Lemon. And the sight was not one I'd forget.

When I'd first met the police receptionist, she'd looked like something straight out of a '50s sitcom: pale blonde hair done up in a chignon, carmine lipstick, cats-eye glasses. She'd even worn a fit-and-flare dress with a cardigan over the top. Although she looked to be about thirty or so, it was hard to tell with supernaturals, and she was definitely supernatural. I wasn't sure what flavor, but her canines were a tad too long, and there was a sparkle in her eye that sometimes made me uneasy.

While her hair was still up in her signature vintage style, she wore not a stich of clothing except a very prim pearl necklace. I swear to goddess, I'd never seen such a bunch of energetic twerking in my life. I hadn't realized witches twerked.

I guess we could dance however we wanted to. I'd stick to something sedate. Like the rhumba.

Lemon paused mid-twerk as she caught sight of me. Her finely penciled eyebrows rose as she slowly straightened and walked toward me. "Well, JJ, it's nice to see you. I hadn't realized you shared your grandmother's enthusiasm for dance, or I'd have invited you along earlier."

"Uh. I don't, really. I just... Here, I brought you these." I thrust a box of Branwen's cupcakes at her.

She grinned. "Fabulous. I'll put it with the other potluck dishes."

I peered at a picnic table which was covered with plates of cookies, brownies, donuts, and even a four-layer coconut cake. I guess dancing skyclad worked up an appetite for sweets.

As Lemon sat the box next to the other goodies, I pointed toward the path. "The, uh, lights. They're... what are they?"

She gave me a knowing look. "You're worried about the creatures inside."

I nodded. "I don't want to be judgy or anything."

She snort-laughed. "I'd be judgy. But don't worry, they're not being harmed."

"They're still imprisoned," I pointed out.

"Uh, yeah. Of course they are. They're pucks."

I gave her a blank look.

She sighed, took out a raspberry and dark chocolate cupcake and took a bite. "Bliss! I forget you're not from around here. Pucks are a type of pixie, and they're malicious as heck. Those little demons are the fae version of piranha. Let them out, and we'd be bones in minute."

My stomach churned. "Ew."

"Yeah. They don't usually cross into our realm because they don't do well in a world with such low levels of magic. Not to mention it's against fae law because, you know, humans. That's why the veil is difficult to pass through. But those little jerks crossed over anyway and nearly decimated an entire herd of dairy cows before we got to 'em."

"Holy bananas. Was the farmer one of us at least?" I couldn't imagine trying to explain the aftermath to a non-magical human.

"Unfortunately, no."

"Then how on earth did you explain it?"

She gave me a wry smile. "Aliens."

"Oh. I guess that would work. So they're basically in prison for their crime?"

"Exactly. And since they are, they might as well make themselves useful. Once they've served their sentence, they'll be released back to the fae." She waved her hand. "But you didn't come here to talk about criminals. Or did you?" She gave me another knowing look and held up a pretty, vintage cut glass decanter. "Cocktail? I know you're the expert in magical cocktails, but I make my own moonshine."

"I don't know about being an expert, but I wouldn't mind one cocktail." There'd be time enough for it to wear off before I drove back to town. Not to mention plenty of food, albeit in mostly sugar form. I kind of wanted to stick around and see what these ladies got up to.

"Oh, you're definitely an expert." She eyed the space around me with narrowed eyes. "Yes, indeed. As I thought. You've inherited Agnes's ability in that department. Still developing, but you've got time. Bet you'll be better than she was."

"I can't read people's auras or whatever to decide what they need." That had been a part of my grandmother's gift.

"Not yet. Like I said, it's still developing. As are the rest of your gifts."

She sounded like she knew about me. "You know what kind of witch I am?" That was something that had stumped even Elvira and Enki.

Lemon glanced at that space again. "Of course. You're an Elemental Eclectic."

I stared at her, my mind racing with a million questions. Was it really that easy? Did she just…know? This whole time? "Why didn't you tell me this before?"

She shrugged as if it were no big deal. "I never looked before. And," she tapped a fingernail against her cocktail glass, "I never had this before. Moonshine makes it work better. Not just any moonshine, of course. Gotta be my particular moonshine. It's magic." She winked.

Of course it was. "I have no idea what this means. Being an Elemental Eclectic."

"Elvira can tell you more than I, but you've inherited a variety of interesting abilities from various portions of your heritage. The cocktail thing from Agnes, although she was a Sea Witch, and you are not. But you will eventually be able to read auras. Your cocktail magic will get even stronger then. I imagine you'll be adept at candle magic, too."

Heat seared through me, and my fingers tingled, a sure sign I was about to have an epic hot flash complete with magical meltdown. I took a deep breath, trying to force it back. I did not have the time. Cool air wafted off the ocean and I suddenly felt better. "How about the blowing stuff up?"

She frowned. "That's an interesting one. There's a touch of Fire Witch in you. That's the Elemental part. Somewhere in your background there's a Fire Witch, but I can't recall any of the Jones women holding that power."

I shrugged. "Probably way back when they were in Scotland or something."

Her expression grew troubled, but only for a brief moment before smoothing out. "Perhaps, but I'm not so sure."

It had to be. There wasn't really any other option. I rubbed my still tingling fingers against my jeans. "What else can you tell me about my magic?" I still had so many questions.

She shook her head. "Sorry, that's all I've got. Not without a lot more…investigation."

"What does that mean?"

She smiled somewhat enigmatically. "Magic, my dear. But not as you know it. Now is not the time, however. Soon, maybe."

"How do you know all this stuff?" She wasn't a witch, that I knew.

"I can see it." She swirled her finger around my face. "There."

"In my aura?"

"Sort of. But it's more than just your aura. Some would say it's your soul. Your true entity beyond the physical."

I stared at her. "What the hell are you?" Then I bit my lip. "Sorry, that was rude."

She laughed. "Not really. To be expected. Perhaps I'll even tell you one day."

"But not tonight."

"Nope. Tonight we've got some drinking and dancing to do." She held out a plastic cup shaped like a martini glass but hot pink, filled to the brim with pale yellow liquid.

I accepted the glass she offered and took a tentative sip. It was sweet, citrusy, with an undertone of herbs. There was a tiny buzz of magic to it, but nothing like the cocktails I made. They just made me feel relaxed, enhancing the natural good work of alcohol.

"This is really good," I told her. The last of the tingling disappeared and I felt almost back to normal again.

"I make my own limoncello, too."

"I'll have to get your recipe." I'd never made much of anything in the kitchen before, but apparently cocktails were my new gig.

"Sure. I'll email it. Now, why don't you tell me why you're really here." Lemon took a sip of her own drink then plucked a lemon bar from the table.

I took a deep breath. "I'm here to talk about a dead guy."

twelve

"You mean the guy they found at Eoinn's?" Lemon asked.

"How many dead guys are there in this town?" It popped out before I could reign it in.

Fortunately, she wasn't offended. Instead, she laughed. "Good point."

I dug around in my purse and handed her the picture of Gilmore Benedict. "Here. This is the guy."

"Yeah, I remember him." She handed me back the picture. "I was just coming out of hot yoga with Abilene Simpson and Molly Tipanny when this guy comes up and asks where he can get cell service." She shook her head. "As if everyone doesn't know normal cell phones don't work here."

They didn't. The magic interfered with the signal. I'd had to buy a special Miracle Bay phone called a Peach—yeah, I know—in order to call or text anyone outside of town. Or inside, for that matter. The only reason I hadn't known about it was I'd never been to town before. Anyone who'd even visited knew about the Peach phones and usually had one to use while inside the magical fog barrier. Which meant the dead guy very definitely hadn't been from around here. But then, we knew that already.

"What'd you tell him?"

"I sent him to the grocery store to get a phone, of course."

"Was he magical?" I asked. Quintero had said he wasn't. Even Eoinn claimed Gil had been mundane, but I wasn't so sure.

She poured herself another drink. "How else would he get in town?"

"As we know, there are other ways."

"And you're trying to figure out those ways. What makes you think I'd know if he was magical or not?"

It was my turn to give her a look. "Please. There is nothing that goes on in this town that slips by you."

She preened. "True." She took a bite of lemon bar and moaned. "That new neighbor of yours sure knows how to bake."

The lemon bars did look good. I decided one wouldn't hurt. I was wrong. The dang thing was beyond delicious. I might have had a second one. Okay, three. "The dead guy," I prodded around a mouthful of citrusy goodness.

"Right. He had magic, but it wasn't... normal."

"What do you mean?"

"She means," said a woman, coming up to the table, "that while he clearly had magic, it was strange. Like nothing I'd ever seen before." The woman was tall and spare, probably about sixty, with salt and pepper hair. She filled her lime green martini glass and took a deep sip.

"Abilene's right," Lemon said. "Strangest magic I ever saw, but he was humming with it."

"So you don't know what he was?" I asked.

Abilene shrugged. "No idea. He could have had rare magic, or he could have been hexed. Hard to tell with these things sometimes."

"What sort of hex?" I asked.

"He could have been non-magical, and someone infused him with magic." Abilene took another sip of her cocktail. "Never seen it done but heard of it."

"Why would someone infuse a non-magical person with magic?" I mused.

"Lots of reasons," Lemon said. "Not necessarily nefarious. Could just be to get him through the barrier, although there are much easier ways."

"Those involve Council approval," Abilene pointed out.

"True," Lemon agreed.

"Would he be able to use the magic for anything other than sneaking into town?" I asked.

"Depends on the spell," Abilene said. "Whether it was residual magic or active magic. Active means he could channel it into something. Residual wouldn't do much but get him through the barrier. Maybe act as camouflage."

"Which was it?" I asked, glancing from Abilene to Lemon and back again.

Abilene shrugged. "No idea. Maybe neither. I could sense the magic and its strangeness, but that was it." She downed her drink in one go. "I'm back at it. You going to join us?"

I froze. "Me?" It came out squeakier than I'd like.

"Why not?"

"I-I'm not really comfortable... skyclad."

She laughed. "You don't have to go skyclad if you don't want to, but it is liberating." She danced off, butt cheeks jiggling, completely unconcerned about her dimpled backside and the cellulite on her thighs. I sort of wished I could be like her when I grew up.

"It was active," Lemon said, reeling me back to the matter at hand.

"What?"

"The magic in your dead guy. Definitely active. It was either a part of him or someone infused him with active magic. Either way, it means he could have channeled it."

"For what?" I asked.

"That's the million dollar question, isn't it?"

"No ideas?"

"Plenty," she said with a shrug. "But none that make much sense."

I picked up a fourth lemon bar. It paired really well with the homemade moonshine and limoncello cocktail. I really needed some of Lemon's recipes. "For example?"

"Back in the '70s, there was this group of bank robbers."

I stared at her, unsure where this was going. "Okay?"

"They hit small town banks all up and down the coast. Nobody could figure out how they got in and out without being detected. In fact, the mundane police still have it listed as an unsolved crime."

"Let me guess. You know what really happened."

She gave me a smug smile. "Yes, I do. Your grandmother and I worked together to discover that the ringleader had kidnapped a young witch and forced her to infuse them with magic. One of the gang channeled it to render the group invisible. Another used it to open the bank vault. They were in and out in minutes without anyone the wiser."

"Whoa. Let me guess. They kept the witch because she had to keep infusing them with magic."

Lemon nodded. "Exactly. The magic wore off after each job, so she'd have to keep renewing it. By the time we found her, they'd nearly burned her out."

"And the gang? You said they weren't caught."

Her smile was only slightly evil. "Oh, not to worry. They were dealt with."

"Um, good." I couldn't help myself. I needed to know. "I thought the Council didn't deal with mundanes. Not their purview and all that."

"They don't usually, but in this instance, these jerks kidnapped a witch, stole magic, and used it for nefarious purposes. The usual legal channels aren't exactly equipped for that."

She had a good point. "They didn't, ah, kill them or anything?"

Lemon snorted. "Don't be absurd. The council doesn't kill people. Especially not mundanes."

Well, that was a relief.

"Now are you joining us or what?"

I was feeling a little fuzzy around the edges with the alcohol and sugar. Probably not a good time to drive. "Sure. For a while."

She pointed at my shoes. "I recommend going barefoot. Better way to connect with the Earth and her magic. Otherwise, do as you will with the rest of your clothes."

"I think I'll keep them on."

She shrugged. "Boring, but suit yourself. Now let's dance."

She cranked the stereo, and everyone shouted and jumped, waving their hands wildly. I'd never seen so many jiggling body parts in my life. No judgment. It was just weird for me who'd grown up in a society where people—middle aged women, especially—were constantly shamed for their bodies. It was going to take a while for me to leave that part behind.

Lemon tossed some sort of powder onto the fire, and the flames shot up higher. A sweet, smoky scent drifted around me, and for a while I lost myself in the music, the dance, and the warm glow of the moon and stars.

As the party wore down, I managed to get my neighbor by herself for a moment. "Hey, Dahlia, how's the new house treating you?" It was lame, but it was all I had.

"Oh, marvelous. I love it. It's simply perfect." She stretched leisurely. "Did you enjoy the evening?"

"It was different, but yes. I wouldn't mind coming again. Just not sure about the skyclad part. For me, I mean."

She shrugged. "It's not for everyone. You could always get a ritual outfit. Something fun and floaty. That way you feel special."

"I like that idea. Thanks." Might as well charge in. "I was wondering, how long have you had your familiar?"

"Oh, not long. He showed up shortly after I arrived in town."

"You didn't have one before?" I asked.

She shook her head. "They're rare, you know."

I did know. Until her, I was the only one in town that had one. Scratch that, I was still the only one who had one because Froggy Kenneth was definitely not a familiar.

"I never thought I'd have one," she continued. "I'm so lucky."

"How'd you know that's what he was?" I asked. "And not, you know, just an ordinary frog." Not that Kenneth *was* an ordinary frog, but I wasn't about to tell her the full truth. I had no idea yet if she was trustworthy.

"He told me, of course. Familiars can speak to your mind."

"How interesting." She was right, familiars did speak directly to your mind, but they spoke to everyone, not just their witch. Anyone magical could hear them. Froggy Kenneth very definitely could not talk. Unless "ribbit" counted as speech. Which meant... what? Someone had made her think Kenneth had spoken to her? Either they'd implanted a memory, or more likely, had somehow spoken directly to her mind in a way that made her think the frog had spoken. Question was, why?

This was going to take a lot more investigation.

thirteen

The lights were still on in the library when I drove by, which was strange because it was getting pretty late. I hoped nothing had happened to Elvira. Worried, I parked in the small lot next to the bike rack—currently occupied with a well-used all terrain bike—and made my way inside.

The Miracle Bay Public Library was located in a mid-century modern building with a wall of windows facing west, giving it an excellent view of the ocean during the day, and a gently curved roof that made it look almost like a spaceship. The interior had a simple, elegant design from the pendant lamps to the wood-framed leather armchairs, all original.

Elvira—resplendent in a yellow velour track suit—was supervising a young person as they shelved books. Her minion looked to be hardly old enough to legally work. They had a head of shaggy, mousey brown hair, pale golden-brown skin, and ears that were ever so slightly pointed. Not enough for full elf, but maybe half.

"Hey, G-ma. Thought you'd have knocked off by now." I slunk into the chair next to her, my worry subsided.

"I'm training my new recruit. Bellamy, this is my granddaughter, JJ. She/her. JJ, this is Bellamy, they/them."

"Hi, Bellamy. Nice to meet you."

Bellamy gave me a shy smile which flashed a tiny dimple in their left cheek. "Hi." They went back to shelving books, but they kept sneaking peeks from under their shaggy bangs as if I was terribly interesting.

I glanced at Elvira with a lifted brow.

"Like you, Bellamy is new to town. They haven't met many witches before."

"I'm three-quarters witch," Bellamy offered shyly. "But I was raised by my grandfather who is an elf. He thought it was time I had exposure to my other heritage."

"Bellamy's witch powers started manifesting recently. Most unusual for one of elf blood to also have witch powers, but there we go. Life is full of mystery and magic."

"Well, if anyone can help you with witch magic, it's my grandmother," I told Bellamy.

Bellamy gave me that shy smile again. "I hope so."

"Why don't you knock off for the night, Bellamy," Elvira said. "It's late, and JJ and I have business to attend to. I will see you in the morning."

Bellamy whispered a shy goodnight and hustled out the door. My guess was the bike in the rack must be theirs.

"Do they live close?"

"Their grandfather, Thorven, just took over the antique and vintage hardware shop down the road." She went behind the desk and switched off the computers, then went around shutting off the lights before ushering me out the door. "The two of them live in the apartment overhead. Much like you."

"When exactly did they arrive?" I asked as she locked the library door.

She shot me a look that told me I hadn't fooled her one bit. "A good three weeks before either your neighbor or your frog."

"He's not exactly my frog," I protested. "So you think it's a coincidence, then?"

"More than likely. Although one never knows. Pays to keep the mind open."

I glanced around, but my car was the only one in the lot and there was no sign of Elvira's Vespa. "Did you walk?"

"Of course. It's hardly far. And going home is all downhill."

"Well, you might as well ride with me. We can talk about what I found out while I drive you home."

"I have a better idea. You can drive me home, then we can hit Twisted Whiskey while we talk."

"I thought they only did flights." Not that I minded whiskey, but I preferred it in cocktail form.

"I had a talk with Yarrow a while back, and she's now offering whiskey-based mixed drinks. You'll like it."

"Sounds great. Although I might have to walk home after."

"Good for the constitution."

Twisted Whiskey was literally across the street from Elvira's bank-turned-home. I often wondered if she'd picked her building based on that or if it were a happy coincidence.

The tasting room was completely covered in wood planking from the floors to the ceiling. The planks on the walls had been painted matte black, while the floors and bar—which extended around the entire room—were natural polished. Simple stools sat along the bar, and a couple of red and gold Karastan rugs warmed the floor.

Tansy ran things behind the scenes, being the master distiller, while Yarrow managed the tasting room. They were both low level kitchen witches, their abilities lending themselves well to their chosen craft. I was excited to try the new offerings.

Over the frothy deliciousness of Yarrow's Cherry Whiskey Sours, I told Elvira the thing that had been on my mind. "Lemon knows what kind of witch I am."

Elvira froze, drink halfway to her mouth. "What? How is that even possible? Why didn't she tell us before?"

"I don't know. She said something about needing moonshine for it to work. The 'it' being her magical ability, I guess."

"Interesting. I've always wondered what she put in that moonshine. What did she say about *your* magic?"

"She said I'm an Elemental Eclectic—whatever that means—with a touch of Fire."

She paused, drink halfway to her mouth. "That's not possible. There isn't a single touch of fire magic in the entire Jones line. She must be mistaken."

Disappointment shot through me. "You think she was wrong about my magic?"

Elvira looked thoughtful. "Maybe. Maybe not. Lemon is…unusual. She is very secretive about her past. Even I have no idea what type of supernatural entity she is. She's even more secretive about her abilities. Although—"

"Although what?" I prodded.

"The eclectic part makes some sense. It would explain your affinity for cocktail magic as well as the fact your magic is all over the place." She shook her head. "But the fire magic? I think she must be wrong." She frowned. "Except I'm not sure Lemon has ever been wrong about anything. She doesn't often share, but when she does, she's scarily accurate. But where could the fire magic have come from?"

"Lemon said there was a way to find out, but it takes some special kind of magic to do it."

Elvira sighed. "Of course it does. Let me try and talk to Lemon. Maybe she'll be willing to work with me."

I nodded, hope warring with fear. I was so close to finding out more about my magic. "Thanks."

"Of course." She squeezed my hand. "Now, what'd you find out about the dead guy?"

I told her everything I'd discovered at the skyclad dance. "It's not much," I admitted.

"No, it's not," she agreed. "But I find it very interesting that someone possibly imbued this Gilmore person with magic. Especially based on Eoinn's visions."

I frowned. "What do you mean?"

"Don't you think it strange that Eoinn would see himself in a relationship with the victim in other timelines? But that the victim had no magic?"

"Not really. Don't magical people date non-magical people?" After all, I'd dated Kenneth pre-frog and he wasn't magical. Granted, at the time I hadn't known I was a witch.

"Not if they live in Miracle Bay. Remember, non-magical people can't just stumble across this place, and Eoinn never leaves. Never would leave. The outside world is too much for him. Too much input. Too overwhelming. The one time he tried, we nearly lost him. He was catatonic for a week. There is no timeline in which Eoinn could have left Miracle Bay to meet anyone. What does that tell you?" She knocked back the last of her cocktail.

"I'm not sure," I admitted. "I guess that the only way he could ever have met Gil was here in town. In all those timelines, someone must have brought him here."

"Unlikely."

I sighed. "Then what is more likely? That someone just stuck some fake memories of faker timelines in Eoinn's head?"

Her expression was grim. "Exactly. I think somebody's been messing with our psychic."

"Are you sure this is a good idea? What if his head explodes?"

"His head is not going to explode, Maude." Harriet rolled her eyes.

"You don't know," Maude insisted, twisting her fingers in her frilly apron covered in pink rosebuds. "We've never tried this before. It could all go horribly wrong."

"Would you lighten up?" Daphne patted Maude on the back. "It can't be that bad if Elvira's got it in her grimoire. Just because *we've* never done it before doesn't mean it can't be done, darlin.'"

"It can be," Stella said. Her voice took on a spooky cast. "I saw it done once. It was a dark night in the summer of 1873..."

"Shut it, Stella," Harriet snapped. "We do not have time for this. Elvira, dear, tell us what to do." She turned to my grandma expectantly.

After our revelation, Elvira and I had collected Eoinn, then headed to the vampires' house. They'd just gotten up and were more than happy to assist in Elvira's plan, whatever that was. She'd been cagey about it.

For his part, Eoinn seemed remarkably calm. He sat at the kitchen table, nursing a cup of black coffee Maude had given him, looking bemused and rumpled. But then bemused was sort of a default for Eoinn.

"How are you so calm?" I asked softly.

"I had a vision Elvira was on her way, so I took an edible just in case."

Oh, boy. I hoped that didn't interfere with whatever spell she was cooking up. I had no doubt there was a spell; I just didn't know how the vampires were involved.

Someone called? Enki strolled into the room as if he owned the place.

"No," I said. "No one did."

Pity. I came anyway. Exciting stuff afoot.

"How do you know?" I demanded.

I'm a familiar, remember? I have my ways.

"Speaking of, I need to talk to you about our neighbor."

"Later." Elvira interrupted me. "Right now, we need to focus on Eoinn and the revealing spell."

A revealing spell made sense. "Why are we having vampires involved in our spell? Won't that interfere with the magic?" I asked.

"Because Eoinn is psychic," Harriet said as if that explained everything. She still wore her blue terrycloth bathrobe, but she wore it like a queen.

Vampires offer a fixed point in time, Enki offered less than helpfully.

"Yeah, that cleared up nothing," I snarked.

"Usually if I suspected that a person's memories had been hacked by magic, a simple reveal spell would show me the truth," Elvira explained as she began pulling items out of her oversized, lime green handbag. "Unfortunately, Eoinn's particular abilities mean that any magical meddling can hide between the threads of psychic 'memories,' making them impossible to unravel with a typical spell."

"With you so far."

"Good." She handed me several fat, white candles. "Set these out in a circle on the floor around the kitchen table." While I did as she instructed, she continued. "Pure witch magic won't work because of the mutable nature of the timelines, however, because vampires are technically dead—"

"Dead-ish," Stella corrected, adjusting her hairnet.

"Of course." Elvira nodded. "Because vampires are technically dead-ish, they create a fixed point in time, the point of their undeaths, allowing for the timelines to be more easily unwoven. While vampires do not have intrinsic magic of their own, they can be involved in the spellwork and become, in a way, part of the spell, acting as anchors of the true timeline."

That was all very wibbly-wobbly, timey-wimey, but it made a strange sort of sense. "This will let us see if Eoinn's psychic memories were tampered with?"

"It will." Elvira sounded convinced. "And if his were, then we can assume your new neighbor's were as well."

Oh, they were, Enki assured her. *There's no way in any timeline that blasted frog is a familiar.*

I was one hundred percent with him on that. "What do we do?"

"Eoinn should remain seated at the table, with the vampires each touching him," Elvira said. "Now, JJ, I need you to mix together a special cocktail to reveal the truth." She pulled several bottles out of her pack and shoved them into my hands. "Eoinn will drink it, and then you and I will cast the spell."

"Uh, sure. Okay. You have a recipe or something?"

She handed me various ingredients, mostly involving lemon. One by one, I mixed them up, all the while visualizing the truth being revealed and whatever was messing with Eoinn's mind washing away. I poured the drink in a coupe glass and handed it to Eoinn. He gave me a watery smile before tossing back the drink. He probably barely tasted it. What a shame.

"Now, JJ, recite this spell with me." Elvira thrust a piece of paper in my hand.

I glanced at it and nodded. "I'm ready."

As am I. For once Enki wasn't being snarky.

Together we chanted out loud:

"Beneath the fog of confusion
behold the threads of that which is true
anchored at the point of undeath.
All but one is false,
meant to deceive and confuse,
but now the eye of the spirit is open
and the truth shall be revealed.
We untangle the threads of falsehood
revealing only truth.
So mote it be."

Energy tingled along my arms and down my spine as the magic took hold. I sucked in a deep breath and opened my eyes.

"Well, that's the freakiest thing I've ever seen," Stella muttered loudly.

"Hush, Stella. Don't be rude," Daphne hissed back.

"Am I wrong? Look at his eyes," Stella snapped.

We all turned to stare at Eoinn who stared back with a blank expression. And sure enough, his eyes glowed an eerie bright blue.

fourteen

"What's wrong with him?" I whispered. I'd never seen anything like the eerie blue glow emanating from Eoinn's eyes. It was straight out of a horror movie. "Eoinn? Are you okay?"

There was no answer. He didn't even twitch.

"He's fine. It's just the spell," Elvira assured us. "Now we can untangle the threads of his memories."

That ought to be a real treat, Enki said with heavy sarcasm.

"Hush your mouth, familiar, or you'll be a frog next," Elvira snapped.

I held back a giggle. "How do we do this?" It was so far beyond my area of knowledge that I felt like I'd been moved from the kiddie pool to shark-infested waters.

"We don't do anything," Elvira said. "They do." She nodded to the Golden Girls.

"That's right honey, you just watch," Daphe said as she passed around silver thimbles to each of the vampires.

They each stuck a thimble on their right middle finger then held it over Eoinn's head. Little sparks danced between the silver thimbles and Eoinn's scalp. They looked for all the world like threads.

Stella hummed something dirge-like as the four of them carefully snagged the glowing energy threads and pulled them from Eoinn, tossing them on the floor where they fizzled out like a match thrust into water. I half expected them to leave scorch marks on the linoleum floor, but they didn't.

"There," Dorothy said, leaning back and tugging off her thimble. "Done."

"And?" Elvira prompted.

Maude squinted at the final energy thread dancing from Eoinn's head. "This is it. The real thread." She beamed at us, cheeks flushed in triumph.

It didn't look any different to me, but then I wasn't a vampire. "What's the real memory?"

"Well, I'm not sure," Maude admitted.

"It's been damaged," Harriet said with a shake of her head. "All those fake memories shoved in there messed up his actual memories. Chances are he may never remember what really happened that day."

"Who could have done this?" I asked grimly. "Could it have been Gil?"

"Not a chance," Stella grunted. "This thing was still active, which means whoever cast it is still alive, feeding it."

"*Why* would anyone do this?" It was, frankly, a little nuts. I couldn't think of any good reason for it.

Figure out the who, you'll find out the why, Enki was quick to point out.

"There are only three newcomers to town," I said. "Bellamy and their grandfather, Thorven, and my lovely nudist neighbor, Dahlia."

"I vote for the neighbor," Stella said. "Running around naked as a jaybird simply ain't natural. Not in this weather."

I didn't necessarily disagree—at least about the weather concerns—but I wasn't sure that enjoying the nudist lifestyle equated to being a murderer. Not to mention after the skyclad evening, I was well aware that several women in town enjoyed a bit of the *au naturale*. Still, Dahlia was the most realistic choice. She'd come here suddenly, her so-called familiar was really my ex-boyfriend turned frog, and she acted a little too over the top. It was time I had another visit with my new neighbor.

Unfortunately for my plans, Dahlia wasn't home. Nor was there any sign of Kenneth. She had, however, made progress on the front porch. Some of the plants had been moved to the backyard while others had been hung or crowded onto the porch railing and steps, leaving more room to move around.

I peeked through the large plate glass window. Normally the room beyond would be a living room, but the previous occupant, Rhodore, had set it up as a store front where he sold his handcrafted, magical skincare products. Other than a stack of boxes in the corner—Dahlia was probably still getting settled—the room remained untouched. Maybe she planned to use it the same way. Or maybe she just hadn't gotten around to dismantling the shelving units. Although, if it were me, I'd keep them and use them as bookshelves.

Unfortunately, with no one home, I'd have to question Dahlia later. Not ideal, but there was no way around it.

Next on my list was Bellamy's grandfather. Why had Thorven suddenly decided to uproot his grandchild and bring them to a completely strange town in a strange land where they knew nobody? Even if Bellamy was part witch, it seemed like an odd choice to make. Particularly with Bellamy at that age when kids were normally spending more time with their friends than their families, graduating school, stuff like that. Of course I had no idea what life was like in the fae realm. Maybe they didn't have high school.

Elvira had told me that Bellamy's grandfather had taken over the local antique and vintage hardware shop, The Antiquarium, so I headed straight there. I hadn't had a chance to check it out yet, since it had closed before I arrived in town, and I was looking forward to it. I loved antiquing.

It wasn't a long walk, and while the day was a bit chilly, it was sunny for once. Witch or not, I could use a bit of vitamin D.

The Antiquarium was located down Benandanti Drive, not far from the Drunken Pixie, in an old hardware store built at the turn of the twentieth century. The stucco front had been painted gray and blue some time ago but was in need of a fresh coat. The large display windows on either side of the door should have displayed wonderous treasures, but instead were dimmed with grime and half covered over by old doors.

I pushed my way in and was immediately hit with the heavy scent of must, dust, and old things. Not unexpected in an antique shop, but it was thicker than usual. Clearly Thorven hadn't had a chance to clean up much since taking over the shop.

Narrow walkways wound between tables stacked with mismatched candlesticks and boxes of glass doorknobs, wonky bookshelves crammed with teapots, and rolled up rugs of indeterminate age. Old paintings and window frames covered in dust leaned against walls, and racks of old clothing were stuffed in corners, while chandeliers from every era imaginable dangled precariously overhead.

I followed the sound of hammering and found Bellamy's grandfather at the back of his shop in a work room as expected. What was not expected was who—or what—Bellamy's grandfather turned out to be.

I'd pictured him an older man, gray-haired, maybe in his sixties or something. Although, doing the math, he could easily be in his forties still if he'd had kids young. The guy in front of me looked barely in his thirties with a tumble of golden curls falling over his forehead and muscles rippling over muscles. This was Bellamy's grandfather? Holy bananas. How was that even possible?

The fae live far longer than humans. Enki suddenly appeared, twining between my feet. It was awkward as heck. *He may look like a—how do you humans say it?—hottie, but he's well over a hundred.*

"Years?" I muttered.

I swear he rolled his eyes. *No minutes. Of course years, you idiot. Fae don't age so quickly.*

I guess not. Because I never would have pegged the guy hammering away at an old dining table as a freaking grandfather. Yikes.

"Excuse me Mr.—uh—Thorven?" I realized I didn't know his surname. Did fae even have surnames? I mean, the Pixietwists did, so I assumed so.

The man glanced up, spearing me with silver eyes. Not gray or a pale blue, but actually silver. He had full lips, cheekbones to die for, and he freaked me out. Not in a good way. Fear shivered up my spine.

Natural reaction to the fae, Enki whispered through my mind. *They are, after all, humans' natural predators.*

That did not make me feel better. I certainly didn't have that reaction to the Pixietwists, but then again, as Theo had pointed out on more than one occasion, they weren't exactly typical.

"Not open yet," Thorven ground out. He sounded almost... angry. "Come back later. Or don't." He went back to his table.

What a cheery guy. "I'm here about Bellamy."

He whipped around and was right in front of me before I could bat an eyelash. I nearly wet myself.

I think I'll make myself scarce. Enki, the coward, slunk away and disappeared under a sawhorse.

"What about Bellamy?" he ground out.

"Um." I licked my lips. "Bellamy works for my grandmother. Elvira? At the library?"

His shoulders relaxed, but only a fraction. "You're Elvira's kin?"

I nodded.

"She's been good to my Bellamy." He stepped back and waved his hammer in the direction of a wobbly looking chair. "Have a seat."

I did, though it was with some trepidation. The thing didn't look nearly sturdy enough to hold my weight. I've never been a small woman. Definitely on the curvy side. The chair gave a slight wobble then settled in.

Thorven went back to his table, although he did put down the hammer. Instead, he picked up a tube of filler and started patching in a spot that looked like a dog had chewed it.

"Why don't you just use magic?" I asked.

He shrugged. "I like to work with my hands. It's soothing."

Which made me wonder what he needed to be soothed from. "It's not the low level of magic here? I heard the fae don't like it."

There was a flash of a wry grin, there and gone so quickly I could have imagined it. "It doesn't help."

"Why would you come here, then?"

He slid me a look. "You're a nosy one."

It was my turn to shrug. "It's in the genes." By all accounts, Agnes had been nosy as heck.

"My access to magic is not what's important."

I nodded. "Bellamy is important. Agnes says they are part witch."

"Three-quarters," he said, swiping a thick layer of goop across the edge of the table. "My wife was a witch. As was my daughter-in-law."

"And they were allowed to live in Elfame?" That was a surprise.

He shook his head. "I lived in the human realm with them until my wife died. My son was grown and no longer needed me, so I returned to Elfame. It was only after my son and daughter-in-law were killed in a car accident when Bellamy was small that I returned here."

"Why did you take Bellamy to Elfame instead of raising them here?"

"Figured it was important that they know the fae part of their heritage. And I thought things were getting better."

"Better?"

His jaw flexed. "The fae do not like those they consider outsiders."

"Ah. But they're more accepting now?"

"They were." He set aside the can of filler and went to work, smoothing out the goop. "Things are slow to change in Elfame, slower even than here in the human realm, and there are those particularly resistant to that change. Unfortunately, after years of forward progress, some were trying to pull us back."

"Let me guess, Bellamy wasn't safe anymore." Elvira had said as much.

He nodded. "I'd heard of Miracle Bay and decided it was the safest place for Bellamy. So we moved here."

"Three weeks ago?"

"Yes. Why?"

"Just curious." Hopefully he didn't see my crossed fingers. "Do you know someone named Gilmore Benedict?"

He frowned. "No. Should I?"

"Not necessarily. It's just… He showed up here in town not long after you did, so I thought maybe you met."

"Nope."

This guy was giving nothing away. "You hear about the murder?"

Was it me, or did his shoulders tense ever so slightly?

"I don't pay attention to gossip."

"A murder isn't exactly gossip," I said dryly.

"I like to keep myself to myself. Now if you don't mind, I'd like to get back to work." As if he'd ever stopped.

"Sure." I got to my feet, the chair wobbling dangerously. "It was nice to meet you. I look forward to checking out the shop once it's open.

He grunted noncommittally and turned his back. Clearly I was dismissed.

So what do you think? Enki asked, rejoining me as I wove my way back to the front of the store.

"I'm not sure," I admitted, keeping my voice low. "He's hiding something, that's for sure, but I don't think it has anything to do with Gil's death." Or Froggy Kenneth for that matter.

Agreed.

I must have given him a look of surprise.

What?

"I can't believe you agreed with me," I said as we stepped out onto the sidewalk.

Well, you can't be wrong all the time.

"Gee, thanks. Your vote of confidence means so much."

Happy to help. And he strolled off as nonchalantly as a cat can. Which is incredibly nonchalant.

As for me, I had a new mystery to ponder. What was Thorven hiding? And was I right? Or was he somehow tied up in murder?

fifteen

"You seem distracted."

I glanced up from my plate of tagliatelle alla Bolognese. The slightest upturn of Con's lips revealed he was amused, not irritated.

"Sorry. I didn't mean to... sorry." My mind had been a thousand miles away. Or rather, down the street with Eoinn.

"No need to apologize. I know you've been dealing with a lot. Spellworking with the Golden Girls is enough to make anyone a little loopy. What's on your mind?"

I sighed, putting my fork down, appetite oddly gone. I rarely lost my appetite, but last night's events had thrown me, especially as Eoinn still hadn't remembered anything about what happened to his memories. Someone had screwed with them, that was for sure. "I'm just so worried about Eoinn and what's going to happen with him. I'm completely baffled over this murder. I can't get my hands on Froggy Kenneth—"

He choked. "Froggy Kenneth?"

I laughed. "That's what Emerald and I have been calling him. Just plain Kenneth doesn't really work, you know?"

"Sure. Why not?" He chuckled, and his ice blue eyes sparkled. He'd taken off his glasses and, while other diners at The Olive Branch shifted uneasily every time they caught sight of them, frankly I loved them, and to my mind it was a sign he was getting more at ease being himself around me. "You'd think Froggy Kenneth would want to be... less froggy."

"You'd think. I mean, he showed up on my doorstep, for crying out loud. But every time I try to grab him, he takes off."

"Maybe we should set a trap," Con suggested.

Now there was a thought. "Maybe. If you think it would work. I have no idea how to catch a frog." Especially one that used to be a person.

"Pretty sure we can figure something out. If nothing else, the Pixietwists might have some ideas. Particularly Marigold. Flora is more her thing, but she's pretty attuned to fauna, too." He took a bite of his lasagna and chewed thoughtfully. "Do you think that Kenneth's appearance has anything to do with the murder? He did lead me to the body, though I'm not sure if it was intentional or not." Probably not. He was a frog, after all.

"I don't know," I admitted. "It seems too much of a coincidence not to be, right?"

"I don't much believe in coincidences," he agreed. "But then this is Miracle Bay. Stranger things have happened."

He had a point there. Either way, I couldn't figure out how Kenneth was tied to Gil's death. Or if the two things were even related. It was frustrating beyond belief. "I keep thinking Gil must have brought Kenneth into town. How else could Kenneth have gotten through the mist?"

"There are other players that could have brought him. Like your new neighbor who claims he's her familiar."

"Yes, there is that. But I just don't see it. Dahlia seems pretty harmless, and Lemon seems to like her." Lemon didn't like many people, so that was a good recommendation as far as I could tell. "Do we know yet how Gil died?"

"He was strangled."

That was a surprise. "He didn't look strangled. Wouldn't there be… signs?"

He took a sip of wine. "Of course, but sometimes they're subtle. In this case, there was some petechia in the eyes and minor bruising around the throat. Nothing you'd have been able to see in the dark."

No doubt Quintero had and simply hadn't told me. Drat her.

"I can't see Dahlia strangling Gil. He was far larger and more muscular than her," I pointed out. "And you know Froggy Kenneth didn't do it."

"Agreed. It would take far more strength than she's got to bring down someone like Gilmore Benedict. And a frog committing that crime is out of the question." His lips twitched in amusement.

"Could be Thorven. He's certainly big and powerful enough." I shook my head, frustrated. "But again, I can't see it. What would be his motive? The fae aren't exactly fond of the human world, so I doubt he has anything to do with Gilmore Benedict. He said he'd never heard of him, not that people don't lie, but I don't think he was lying…"

Con laid his hand over mine. "Why don't we put this whole business aside for now and focus on something else."

I used my free hand to pick up my fork again. "Like?"

There was that amused twist to his lips again. It made the adorable dimple in his cheek flash. "Oh, I don't know, but I bet we can think of something." His voice was a low rumble that did things to my insides.

Was it hot in here? Or was it just me?

The next morning, I hopped in the shower and did a quick cleansing and protection routine I'd read about in Biddy McGraw's journal. Using a simple lemon honey salt scrub I made myself, I gave my skin a good polish. As I did, I visualized the negativity clinging to me was sloughed off, the water washing it down the drain, leaving behind a soft layer of protection. Anything harmful would slide right off

After dinner, Con and I had a romantic walk on the beach. When he walked me to my door, his kisses were hot and sweet and left me breathless. I'd have invited him in if he hadn't gotten a call from Quintero. Drat her.

I toweled off and dressed in simple jeans, boots, and a Smash the Patriarchy t-shirt with a cardigan over top. Coffee in hand, I strolled down to Crystal Gardens, hoping to catch both Pixietwists before Theo went to work. Luck was with me.

"Well, look who the black cat dragged in," Theo said from her perch atop a step ladder where she was arranging a display of pyramid-shaped crystals.

"Better not let Enki catch you saying that," I warned.

She snorted. "What brings you around so early?"

I glanced over to where Marigold was doing her usual flit between her plants, spritzing them while singing slightly off key. "I needed to ask the two of you about catching a frog."

Theodosia stared at me. "Did you say catching frogs?"

"A frog. One. I told you about my ex."

"You did."

"And that he's in town."

"Sure, everyone knows."

Great. Wonderful. "Well, I need to catch him so Elvira can help me turn him back, but he's not exactly cooperating."

"You'd think he'd want to get his human form back," Theo said, descending the ladder, her black and pink wings fluttering slightly to steady her.

"Right? But every time I try to grab him, he runs—or rather hops—off."

"You catch more flies with honey," Marigold sang, missing a fern with her spritzer and hitting me in the face. Fortunately, it was just water, and I dabbed it off with the hem of my t-shirt.

"You mean manure," Theo corrected. "Flies prefer manure."

Marigold blinked wide eyes. "Do they?"

"Yes, dear." There was only a tiny bit of snark in Theo's tone. "Bees and ants like honey, flies like guano."

"Huh. How odd. Why would anyone prefer that to honey?" Marigold looked completely baffled. "Well, if that's what they like. There you go."

"I'm not sure how this helps me," I said with a frission of frustration. "Kenneth is a frog, not a fly."

"Frogs like flies," Marigold said with maddening logic.

"But Kenneth isn't really a frog," I pointed out. "He's a person trapped in a frog's body. I seriously doubt sticking some manure out is going to help me capture him." So much for Con's theory that the Pixietwists could help.

"That's even better." Mari clasped her hands under her chin. Her fingernails were painted green and gold to match her wings. "So easy!"

"Is it?" It hadn't been easy so far.

"Oh, yes. All you need is one of Branwen's honey lavender cupcakes and some tea."

"Tea?" I repeated, completely baffled.

"Not ordinary tea," Theo assured me. "Mari has some very special tea, don't you Mari?"

"Do I?" Mari frowned in confusion.

"Yes, of course you do. You grow it in your garden," Theo prompted.

Mari's face brightened. "Oh, yes, I remember. You go get the cupcake. I'll make tea."

"Right now?" I asked, a bit surprised. I'd figured she would need time to set up... I don't know. A spell or something.

"No time like the present," Theo said bracingly. "Branwen will be open by now. I'll help Marigold with the tea. See you back here in a few."

With a shrug, I headed out the door and down to Branwen's. Sure enough, she was open, the scents of vanilla and cinnamon greeting me in a rush of sugary happiness.

"Oh, good, you're back," Branwen said drily.

"Anyone would think you didn't want to make money," I snarked.

"I'd rather have magic. What do you want?"

"According to Marigold, I need a honey lavender cupcake."

"Mab protect us, what's she up to now?"

I told her about Marigold's plan—such as it was—to catch Froggy Kenneth. "Do you think it'll work?"

"How would I know? I'm not the one turning people into frogs. Although I did once turn someone into a goat."

I blinked. "That sounds like a story."

"Another day, maybe." Her expression turned stony, and I knew I wouldn't get anything out of her on that front.

I turned to go, then I had a thought. I turned back around. "You know the statue of you in the roundabout?"

"Sure."

"Is there something special about it? You know, other than it being gold and of you?"

Her expression was flat, not even a twitch. But was it just me, or did her shoulders tense ever so slightly?

"Not that I know of. It's just a statue. Why?"

I shook my head. "No reason. See you later."

"Sure. Later."

I returned to the Pixietwists' as confused as ever. Gilmore Benedict had been very interested in that statue. Why? Also, I was certain Branwen was hiding something about the statue, but what?

The cousins met me in front of their shop with a pot of tea, a shallow saucer, and a small dessert plate.

"What are those for?" I asked, clutching the small pink box holding the honey lavender cupcake. I wished I'd bought two. I could really use a cupcake right about now.

Theo handed me the dessert plate and a butter knife she pulled from her pink combat boots. I'd heard of people keeping pocketknives in their boots, but a butter knife? "Take off the wrapper and cut the cupcake into small pieces."

"Uh, sure."

While I did that, Theo carefully set the saucer on the sidewalk, and then Mari poured tea in it with great concentration. The tea had a very fragrant herbal scent that made me feel a bit woozy. The whole thing was beyond bizarre. She waved at me, so I put my cupcake-laden plate next to the saucer. Theo then pulled a small velvet pouch from between her boobs and took out half a dozen clear crystals, each hardly bigger than a kernel of corn. She placed them in a ring around the saucer and plate.

As if sensing my burning question, she said, "Once your frog takes the bait, these will form an energy cage around him. We'll be able to capture him."

I wanted to point out that he was not *my* frog, but it seemed like a waste of breath. Instead, I said, "What do we do now?"

Marigold hugged the teapot to her chest. "Now we wait."

sixteen

Waiting had never been my strong suit. I also wasn't entirely convinced that Froggy Kenneth would be lured by a cupcake and a saucer of weird herbal tea. Human Kenneth had always been a bit of a snob when it came to food and beverage. He'd avoided sugar (not for health reasons but because it was fashionable) and waxed poetic about wine—although he always seemed to order wine that tasted more like gasoline than anything resembling a grape.

The three of us—Theo, Marigold, and me—stood inside their shop, peering around the giant amethyst geode in the window, waiting for the trap to do its trick. Theo had even called into work after declaring, "There's no way I'm missing this."

Honestly, I didn't know that there would be anything *to* miss. Even if the trap worked and we caught Kenneth, I still had to figure out how to turn him back into a person. Or as much of one as he'd ever been.

"Here he comes," whispered Theo, hands clenched with excitement.

I glanced around and didn't see a thing. "Where?"

"There." She pointed up the street in the direction of the beach. "Just passing the bookstore."

Movement caught my eye, and I squinted, wondering if I needed glasses. Sure enough, there came a frog wearing a bowtie which was beginning to look a little worse for wear. He hopped across the street and came right up to our trap.

We crossed our fingers and held our breaths. I could practically feel Marigold buzzing beside me. This was it. Would he take the bait?

His tongue shot out as if testing the air. He edged closer to the plate bearing the chopped-up cupcake. He was still on the outside of the ring of crystals. Would he notice them? And if he did, would he realize what they were? Probably not. I hoped not. He wasn't magical, after all. He'd probably think they were just rocks.

He moved closer to the plate. His back foot hit one of the crystals and sent it skittering about an inch. He turned to give it a confused look. I hadn't known it was possible, but his eyes widened, and he turned to leap away from the plate. Crap! He knew it was a trap!

As he turned, his foot slipped on a bit of moss growing between the cracks of the sidewalk. He lost his balance and tumbled backward right into a glob of purple frosting. Immediately, bright white light shot from each of the six crystals, forming an energy cage around him, trapping him inside with the cupcake and tea. I swear if a frog could show rage, he did. Froggy Kenneth was caught at last.

Once we had Froggy Kenneth trapped, it was easy enough to stick him in a cardboard shoebox and haul him back to the bookshop. No doubt he thought it was undignified, but it wasn't my fault he kept running off.

I also sent Elvira a quick text: THE FROG IS IN THE BUILDING.

Her reply was quick: BE RIGHT THERE.

I arrived back at the shop—Pixietwists in tow—just as Emerald strolled up, a green velvet bag embroidered with a peacock over one shoulder. She eyed my little entourage with amusement. "What's going on?"

I nodded to the box. "Finally caught Kenneth. Elvira is on her way."

"Oh! Unfrogging time! Let me get the door."

"Unlock the back door, will you? I'll tell Elvira to come on up when she gets here." I relocked the front door and left the sign showing the store was closed and led everyone up to the former meditation room on the second floor. It was now in the process of being turned into Emerald's tarot reading room, but it was the best spot for what we planned to do, and I knew she wouldn't mind.

Theodosia clomped over and dragged Emerald's tarot reading table and chairs into the corner, leaving us space for whatever ritual would unfrog Kenneth. I placed the box on the floor, not sure what else to do with it. It wobbled a little as Kenneth jumped around, trying to get out.

Marigold peered down at the box. "It's like he doesn't want to be human again, silly frog."

Theo shook her head. "Idiot."

"He really is," I agreed. "I don't know if it's the frog brain taking over or if it's just him being his usual stubborn self."

"Could be he's worried you'll turn him into something worse this time," Emerald said as she entered the room.

"What's worse than a frog?" I asked.

She shrugged. "I dunno. A cabbage?"

"That would definitely be worse than being a frog," Theo agreed.

"I like cabbages," Mari mused. "They're lovely. Very interesting energy."

The rest of us stared at her, but she paid us no mind, completely absorbed in the increasingly shifting box. Kenneth really didn't like being in there. Not that I blamed him, but it was the best I could do. We needed to get him back to himself before it was too late, and he wasn't cooperating.

The back door banged, and footsteps tromped on the steps. Elvira was here.

She appeared in the doorway, resplendent in a raspberry velour track suit and carrying an enormous patent leather handbag the color of a blueberry. She stared at the box which had leapt an inch off the floor. "Excellent. Shall we get started?"

Elvira shoved the box to the side then pulled several items from her bag and set them on the floor next to the box: a silver pendant, an oyster shell, a bag of what looked like ground-up herbs, matches, a handful of crystals, a saltshaker, and a cobalt spray bottle. It was quite a collection.

"First, we have incense made especially for undoing hexes," she said, dumping some of the herbal mixture into the oyster shell. "Rue, hyssop, sage, salt, frankincense, and some other stuff."

I wanted to ask what the "other stuff" was but figured now was not the time.

She placed the oyster shell in the exact center of the room then handed me the matches. "When the time comes, you'll light the incense."

I nodded. "Okay."

Next, she placed a ring of crystals around the incense. The crystals were dark, sort of a greenish black with a rainbow hue. Reminded me of an oil slick, but a lot prettier. "Labradorite is a stone of transformation."

Well, that seemed like a good choice. What with needing to transform a frog back into a human and all.

Finally, she set the spray bottle next to the shoebox and laid the amulet on top of the box. Then she picked up the saltshaker. "Emerald, you join JJ outside the ring of labradorite. The three of us will form a sort of triangle."

Emerald nodded and stepped closer so that she was at a right angle to me. She took a deep breath and shook her hands as if trying to release energy.

"What about us?" Theo asked.

"Since you're not witches, you need to be outside the circle," Elvira said. "However, I'd like you to stand at either side of the door just in case."

I wasn't sure what the "just in case" meant, and I hoped I didn't find out any time soon. Theo and Mari took up their positions on either side of the door, looking like a bizarrely cute set of bodyguards.

Elvira tilted the shaker so that salt trickled out and walked a circle around Emerald and me. "This circle is a sacred space. Nothing in. Nothing out. So mote it be."

"So mote it be," Emerald and I echoed.

Though it was true there were fancier ways to cast and circle, calling up the corners and whatnot, Elvira had always said magic was about intent. Biddy McGraw often claimed the same in her journal. Technically, you didn't even need words to use magic—look at me turning Kenneth into a Frog—but they helped a witch focus.

The minute the circle of salt was complete, an electric shiver went through me. There was no doubt I was in the presence of powerful magic.

Elvira took her place in the circle, forming a triangle between the three of us. "Emerald, take the frog from the box. Hold the frog in one hand and the amulet in the other."

Emerald winced but did as she was told. Keeping a firm grip on the amulet, she lifted the lid with one hand and quickly snagged Froggy Kenneth before he could jump out. He wriggled wildly in her hand, trying to escape.

"JJ, light the incense," Elvira commanded.

I struck a match and touched the flame to the small pile of dried herbs in the oyster shell. They burned for a brief moment, then died to ambers, fragrant smoke drifting from the shell. Froggy Kenneth immediately stopped struggling.

Elvira nodded as if she'd expected that reaction. "You can put him down now in the center of the crystals."

Emerald carefully set Kenneth down next to the smoking oyster shell. "Now what?"

"Give the amulet to JJ. JJ, you tie it around his neck."

He didn't exactly have a neck, but I took the amulet from Emerald, squatted next to Kenneth, and tied it around what would be his neck if he weren't a frog. I was about to stand back up, but Elvira stopped me.

"Pick up the spray bottle and give him a spritz."

I blinked. Seriously? This was the weirdest ritual. Still, I picked up that bottle and sprayed Kenneth right in his froggy face.

He glared at me and let out a hiss. I didn't even know frogs could hiss.

"Now join hands," Elvira said.

I stood up, and the three of us joined hands.

"Focus on the result we want," Elvira said, "and repeat after me."

Emerald and I exchanged glances. I closed my eyes and pictured Kenneth back in his human form.

Elvira cleared her throat. "The hex is cast, the lesson learned. Return this one to his true form. As we will so mote it be."

It seemed too easy, but as Emerald and I repeated the words, energy swirled around us, lifting our hair as if dancing on the wind. The hair on my arm raised with static electricity, and my hearing went dull like it does right before your ears pop. Then everything went still.

Just like at the restaurant when I turned Kenneth into a frog, there was no thunderclap or swirling vortex or anything else exciting. One minute Kenneth was a bowtie wearing frog, and the next he was a very naked man with a drooping bowtie and a magical amulet around his neck. He stared at me, and the malevolence in his eyes was enough to make a lesser woman quail.

Okay, fine, it made me quail.

Emerald was made of sterner stuff. She tossed Kenneth the tablecloth off her reading table. "Put this on. You're freaking everybody out." To me she said, "Remind me to burn that later."

"What the hell is going on?" Kenneth wrapped the tablecloth around his hips and lifted his foot to step out of the circle. Instead, light shot up and he let out a howl. "What the *hell*?"

"Language," Elvira snapped. "You can't leave the circle until we clear it, you nincompoop. Give me a minute." She lifted her hands to dismiss the circle.

The door slammed open, and a naked woman appeared. "Stop!"

seventeen

Dahlia stood in the doorway, naked as a jaybird, bosoms heaving with exertion. "Oh, you already did it."

"Drat. I'm out of tablecloths," Emerald muttered.

"Yes," I said, stepping toward Dahlia. "We undid the spell that made Kenneth a frog. But you knew about that, didn't you?"

She sighed, shoulders drooping. "Yeah, I did."

I crossed my arms. "I think you'd better explain yourself. Who are you really, and what's going on? What do you have to do with Kenneth?"

"I'm his girlfriend," she admitted. "Or at least I was."

"Shut up, Dahlia," Kenneth snapped.

"You should take your own advice," Elvira said with infinite calm. "Unless you'd like me to zip your lips? Literally."

Kenneth blanched and shut his lips. Figuratively. I hadn't taken him for being that smart.

I stared at Dahlia. This was the woman he'd dumped me for? I'd been pissed when he'd done it. Obviously. I'd turned him into a frog. Now? I honestly, I felt sorry for her more than anything. "I thought you were from some commune back east."

"Oh, I am. I grew up there. But then I met Kenneth online, and he convinced me to move in with him. So I moved into his apartment in Portland a few months ago. And, well…"

She'd lived with the guy? He was worse than I thought. I was feeling less guilty about the frog situation. "Go on."

"I feel real bad about it," she said. "I didn't realize at first that he was dating you. He told me he was single." She shot him a glare. "And then when I found out, he claimed he'd planned to break up with you for a long time but just felt sorry for you."

"What a friggin' liar," Emerald muttered.

Kenneth went to open his mouth, but Elvira shot him a warning look, and he shut it.

"I know that now," Dahlia sighed. "But honestly, I thought he was so great. Anyway, he told me he was meeting you for lunch so could break up with you."

"He definitely did that," I admitted.

"When Kenneth went missing after his lunch with you, I did a spell. Found him at a park near the restaurant and realized what happened."

"You did? How?" I asked.

She shrugged. "My line comes into magic young. We're not very powerful, not like yours. You've got to have real power to transmute a person into an animal. Big magic. I don't have that kind of magic. Not even close. I knew I had to find you to get you to turn him back."

"Wait." I held up my hand. "*How* did you know I'd done it? It could have been anybody."

"Please," she scoffed. "You're the only other witch he was dating. I'm sorry about that, by the way. Like I said, I had no idea you were seeing each other, and when I found out, I gave him an ultimatum."

"He chose you," I said without rancor. "But that doesn't explain how you knew about me being a witch."

"Well, he told me of course. Or rather, I found texts in his phone that told me."

I stared at Kenneth who all but growled. "How did *you* know about me? I didn't even know about me!"

Kenneth slid a look to Elvira. "The old witch knows."

"Careful, mister," Elvira warned.

"Elvira?" I turned to look at her. "What is he talking about?"

"I honestly have no idea. I don't—oh."

"What?" I practically shrieked. I was getting really annoyed with everyone but me knowing what was going on.

She squinted at Kenneth. "I couldn't tell until he was out of frog form, but he's an enchanter."

"A what?" I had no idea what she was talking about.

"An enchanter," Emerald repeated. "They've got low level magic themselves. Nothing much to write home about. Enough to coerce people into doing what they want. You usually find them selling used cars or in politics. But they're always wanting more. More magic. More power."

"Which wouldn't be a problem," Elvira chimed in, "except for the fact that they have the ability to drain other supernatural beings of their magic and use that magic for themselves."

Dahlia's eyes widened. "And their favorite magic is that of witches. Oh, my goddess, that explains everything."

"It does?" I really didn't see how. And then it hit me. "Wait a minute, are you saying this slimeball only dated me because he knew I come from a line of witches?"

Several heads nodded at once. Kenneth only looked pissed.

"But I hadn't come into my power," I protested.

"He was waiting," Elvira said. "Biding his time. Our line, like most, come into magic in middle age, so he knew it was only a matter of time."

Dahlia propped her hands on her hips. "But he got impatient. Six months, and you still hadn't manifested any powers, so he decided to ditch you for me." She looked pretty angry about it. Not that I blamed her.

"He didn't realize that the very day he dumped me, my birthday, was the day I'd get my powers." I shook my head. "Oh, Kenneth, you really are a dumbass."

Kenneth let out a string of cuss words that would make a longshoreman blush. Elvira snapped her fingers and his mouth zipped shut. Literally.

"Don't worry. It's temporary," she said. "Unless I decide it's not."

Kenneth went pale as a ghost.

I turned to Dahlia. "You really didn't realize any of this?"

She shook her head, long blonde hair sliding over bare shoulders. "I honestly didn't. I didn't even know you were a witch when I gave him the ultimatum. And then when I figured it out because of the whole frog thing, I didn't initially realize what his plan was. I didn't find that out until I got into his phone later." She glared at Kenneth. "I figured I could come to town and pretend he was my familiar until I tracked you down. That proved easier than expected. Then I could convince you to change him back. I mean, I figured you were pretty pissed at him, and rightfully so. He treated you badly."

"He didn't treat you very well either," I pointed out.

She scowled. "Good point. Kenneth, we are broken up."

He made a muffled mumbling sound of outrage, but his lips were still sealed so we couldn't understand him.

"Why did he keep hopping away when I tried to catch him?" I demanded. "Didn't he want to get turned back?"

She shrugged. "I think the frog brain was asserting itself. Like he needs help with that. It took me so long to find you that he was in that form longer than he should have been."

That explained one thing. "What about the murder? He led me straight to the body."

"I don't know anything about that."

Oddly, I believed her. I turned to Kenneth. "Well?"

Elvira snapped her fingers again, and Kenneth's lips unzipped. He opened his mouth, clearly about to blast us, but she gave him a look. That was enough.

He gave me a saccharine sweet smile. "I didn't kill anybody. I was a *frog* remember."

"You led me to the body," I reminded him.

He shrugged. "Coincidence. I honestly had no idea the body was there. I was trying to get away from you."

"Why would you do that?" I demanded.

He sighed. "Dahlia's right. My brain was a little foggy and I kept forgetting I wasn't supposed to be a frog. Anyway, I was trying to get away from you and just…ran into the guy. Er, corpse."

That answered that, I guessed. But I still had a lot more questions.

"What about messing with Eoinn's mind? His memories?" I demanded, turning to Dahlia.

Dahlia shook her head. "I had nothing to do with that. I don't have enough power to mess with somebody's head, even if I had a good spell for it. The most I could do was make them forget something for five minutes. Not exactly useful."

"And you?" I turned to Kenneth.

"What possible reason could I have? Again, I was a frog. Most of my time as a... I don't remember much of the last few months."

"But you did try to steal *our* power," I pointed out.

A crafty expression crossed his face, and he shrugged. "You weren't using it."

I could have smacked him, but I figured ignoring him was the better course of action. Instead, I turned to Elvira. "What do we do with him?"

"He's guilty of attempted theft of magic. It's a serious crime. The council will deal with him."

He turned red, then white, then red again. "The council has no authority over me. They have no right. They have—"

Elvira snapped her fingers, and blessed silence fell.

Once the witch council had been called, Kenneth was toted away, and Dahlia had gone back to her house, the rest of us gathered in the bookstore's cafe for much-needed coffee. The spell had been tiring as had the emotional toll of confronting Kenneth and discovering the truth behind one of the events that had set my life on a totally new trajectory. A much-improved one, to be honest.

"JJ, what's this?" Theo said, plucking a piece of paper off the counter. It was a photo I'd printed out.

"That's Gilmore Benedict, the murder victim," I said. "I printed that off to show around, see if anyone knew him."

"This isn't Gilmore Benedict," she said, slapping the photo down on the counter. "This is Gilvain."

Marigold gasped. "Oh, no."

"Gilvain? Like Cher?"

Theo blinked. "What?"

"No last name? Never mind. Never heard of him," I said. "You?" I asked Emerald.

"Nope." She shook her head.

"Nor have I," Elvira admitted.

"He's bad. Real bad," Mari whispered.

I glanced at Theo who nodded. "He is extremely bad. The worst. He's one of the current fae king's enforcers."

Con was an enforcer for the witch council, but the way Theo said it, I didn't think the fae enforcers were quite as… nice.

"I think we're going to need a little more than that," Emerald said, setting out the coffees for everyone.

"One of the reasons Mari and I left Elfame year ago was because things had gotten, well, dark."

"Darker than usual," Mari muttered, her wings twitching erratically.

Theo wrapped an arm around her cousin and gave her a gentle squeeze. "When Prince Hefydd came to power, he and his minions were into this pure blood nonsense. He sent his enforcers around to imprison anyone who didn't agree with him, anyone who stood up to him, anyone who wasn't *pure*. That was a problem for Mari and me because our great-great-grandmother was human."

That was news. I hadn't known that.

"We figured it would be safe here because the realms can't be crossed. Not anymore," Mari whispered.

"At least not en masse," Theo agreed.

"What does that mean?" I asked.

"Ah, I know about this," Elvira said. "Centuries ago, the fae could easily cross back and forth between their realm and ours, no artifact needed. It was simply part of their magic. Entire armies could move back and forth without a problem. It became a problem when a fae prince—not Hefydd but one of his ancestors, Odefur—decided to use that ability to conquer the human realm for himself."

"She's right," Theo said. "The only reason he didn't succeed is because a coven of witches and other powerful supernatural entities gathered together and stripped the fae of that ability and transfer it into an artifact."

"A mirror," Elvira supplied. "It was the moment the first witch council was created."

"Without access to the mirror, the fae could no longer pass easily between realms," Theo continued. "Odefur sent his enforcers into the human realm to obtain the mirror and reclaim the fae ability to travel between realms."

"Only that first council was smarter than the fae gave them credit for." Elvira grinned wickedly. "They hid the mirror so well, no one today even knows where it is."

Theo nodded. "The fae can only cross in small numbers and at great cost. You really have to want to be here to face that."

Like Bellamy and their grandfather. "I don't see the problem. If the magic was nullified and the mirror lost, then they can't get to our realm to conquer it anymore," I said.

"Unless Hefydd, who is now king, gets his hands on it. Then we're in real trouble," Theo said grimly. "No doubt that was why Gilvain was here, to find the mirror and take it back to Hefydd in Elfame. Good thing somebody got to him first, or we'd all be screwed."

"But why would he come here to Miracle Bay?" I asked.

"Because this is where the mirror is," Elvira said softly.

I turned to her with wide eyes. "What? Why? How?"

"Because the ancient coven that nullified it was your bloodline," she said. "Jones women hid the mirror. Initially in Scotland, then on the East Coast, and eventually they brought it here to Miracle Bay."

If my jaw could have hit the floor, it would have. "Where is it?"

"I don't know," she admitted. "I don't even think Agnes knew. It was hidden here by Isabelle Jones, the witch that helped Branwen create Miracle Bay, and it hasn't been seen since. No one knows where it is."

That didn't sound good. Felt like something I should rectify at some point, but right now I had more pressing matters. Like a murder to solve.

"There are two other people who crossed the realms at the same time as Gilvain," I said.

"Bellamy and their grandfather, Thorven." Elvira sounded resigned.

I nodded. "I think it's time they explained a few things."

Elvira laid a hand on my arm. "Be careful, JJ. The fae are powerful beings. To go up against one—" She shook her head, not finishing, but I got the picture. It could go very bad.

Marigold unclipped a chain from around her neck. From it dangled a little glass vial filled with bits of flowers and herbs. One of her fairy charms. She held it out to me. "This will help protect you. I hope."

Great. What a lovely vote of confidence. "Thanks, Mari." I straightened my shoulders. "Send me all the good vibes."

I was definitely going to need them.

eighteen

I knew confronting Thorven by myself was a dumb move, so I took Elvira with me. Enroute, she called Con. We'd decided against informing Quintero until we knew for sure what was going on. My growing suspicion could be wrong. Sadly, I doubted it.

We found Thorven in his shop, sanding down the table he'd been working on earlier.

He looked up when we entered and grimaced. "What do you want?"

"We need to talk about why you're here in Miracle Bay." I gave him my sternest look. I doubt it fazed him.

"We already had this discussion." He scowled at me. Definitely not cowed.

"Let's have it again, why don't we," Elvira said, taking a seat on the same rickety chair I'd sat on before, making it clear she wasn't going anywhere.

I slapped the picture I'd printed of Gilvain on the table. "I also want to talk about him."

"What about him?" Thorven played nonchalant really well, but his gaze flicked to the image of the murder victim and the muscles around his mouth tightened just a fraction. I'd have never noticed if I wasn't looking.

I tapped the photo. "This is the murder victim. The one I told you about before. Gilmore Benedict, remember?"

"Sure. And I told you I didn't know that name."

I held back a smirk. "That's because you know his real name. Gilvain."

There was a fraction of a hesitation. "And? I still don't know him."

"Don't you? That's funny. You see we recently found out that, like you, Gilvain was fae." I watched him closely.

He gave nothing away. "Just because we're both fae doesn't mean I know him. There are millions of us. Do you know every human?"

"In the fae realm, sure, there are millions," I agreed. "Except here in Miracle Bay there are what?" I turned to Elivra. "A hundred?"

"Less." A small smile curved her lips, staring straight at Thorven. "There are fifty-three. Including you and Bellamy."

The Pixietwists were two and Quintero, as an elf, made three. I wondered who the others were. Not that it mattered right then. "Fifty-three is certainly a small enough number I'd expect you'd know each other. Or at least know of each other."

"Like you said, we're new in town," he gritted out.

"Sure," I agreed. "So new that you literally arrived the same time as Gilvain."

"We arrived two weeks earlier," he snapped.

I widened my eyes in fake surprise. "How did you know when he arrived?"

"You told me," he said.

"Ah, but I didn't. I never mentioned the date he arrived. Only that he was new in town, like you." I gave him my smuggest look. Petty, but I was tired of being lied to.

"Coincidence," he snapped.

"I don't believe in coincidences." Elvira's tone was stern.

"Believe what you like. It's no matter to me." He shrugged and went back to sanding his table.

Just then the door banged open and Eoinn burst in, Con hot on his heels. The red-headed psychic was out of breath and waving his arms around wildly. "I remember! I remember!"

"Remember what?" Elvira asked. "Deep breath, Eoinn. What do you remember?"

Eoinn glared at Thorven. "I remember that it was the dead guy who messed with my memories."

Somehow that didn't surprise me. "But why?"

"I don't know," he admitted. He whirled on Thorven. "But I do remember that *you* were there."

Con's voice was a dangerous rumble. "I think you have some explaining to do."

Thorven heaved a sigh and sank into the chair next to Elvira, head in hands. "I was only trying to protect them."

"Who?" I asked.

He glanced up. "Bellamy, of course."

His grandchild. Of course. I sat down too. "What happened?"

He ran his fingers through his pale blond hair. "In the Fae Realm, it does not pay to be... different."

I nodded. "I have some friends who are fae. They told me. Your king doesn't like people who don't fit his definition of 'pure blood.' And Bellamy is part witch, right?"

He nodded. "Not just that, but as you know, Bellamy doesn't fit the current standard definition of gender."

Elvira snorted. "Who does?"

"I would have thought the fae weren't so worried about things like that," I said. After all, the fae I'd met had been open and kind people. They didn't care about things like gender or sexual orientation. In fact, I didn't think anybody in Miracle Bay did. Not that I'd met anyway.

"They are much more concerned with it than humans," Thorven said. "At least they are now that Hefydd and his cronies have taken over. It had become too dangerous for Bellamy to remain there. I needed to keep them safe."

"So you brought them here," I said. "But what has that got to do with Gilvain?"

Thorven's expression grew dark. "One cannot leave the fae realm these days without Hefydd's approval. And he does not give it easily. He agreed to let me go, but there was a price."

"Which was?" Con prodded.

"There is an object here that would allow Hefydd to return with his soldiers to the human realm. I was to assist Gilvain in retrieving it."

The object was, of course, the one Elvira had told me about. The mirror.

"Gilvain worked for the king?" I knew the truth, but I wanted his side of things.

He nodded. "One of the worst of Hefydd's enforces. They're all brutal, but he enjoys his work a little too much."

"What happened?" Con prodded.

"I was to come through the veil first with Bellamy, find the object in question. Once Gilvain arrived, we were to steal the object, and Gilvain would return to Elfame with it." He scowled. "But I knew that would not be the end. Hefydd would use it to conquer this world just as he conquered ours. Then there would be no safe place anywhere for Bellamy or anyone else who Hefydd and his minions view as less than."

Which likely meant humans, too. Cold fingers tripped down my spine. "Why mess with Eoinn, though?"

"Because he was the only one in town who might be able to figure out what happened, thanks to his visions. Hefydd did not want the council to realize we'd stolen the object until it was too late. We needed to change Eoinn's visions to cloud the truth and Gilvain had that ability. I allowed him to go ahead with that part of the plan in order to protect myself," he admitted. He glanced at Eoinn. "I'm sorry about that."

"I understand," Eoinn said softly. "You needed to remain free to protect Bellamy."

Thorven nodded. "I never planned to allow Gilvain to obtain the object, never mind return it to Elfame and Hefydd's control. I also knew he would never give up and, as long as he was here, this world would always be in danger. So once he'd tweaked Eoinn's memories, I took his magic from him and strangled him."

"Is that why we couldn't detect any magic?" I asked.

He nodded.

"Would the draining have looked like a hex?"

He looked me straight in the eye. "Yes, probably. That was the plan. And before you think I'm sorry, I'm not. I would do it again a thousand times to keep Bellamy safe."

I actually understood that. I didn't necessarily approve of it, but I understood it.

Con sighed as he rose from his seat. Reluctantly he said, "Thorven, you are under arrest for the murder of Gilvain of Elfame."

"Seriously, Con? He saved all of us," I pointed out. "If he hadn't killed that evil fae, we'd probably all be dead. Or enslaved. Or something equally awful."

"He still killed someone," Con said. "It's the law, and I'm sworn to uphold it. The judge will decide his fate."

That sounded ominous.

Thorven stood with resignation and held out his hands so Con could cuff him. "It's all right, Ms. Jones. He's doing what he has to do, just as I did." He turned to Elvira. "Promise me you'll look after Bellamy."

She placed a gentle hand over his. "Always. I swear it." Something like lighting zipped between their hands as if magic sealed her oath. Maybe it did. The fae took words very seriously.

"Wait," I said. "Did you ever find this object you were looking for?"

Thorven shook his head. "Honestly, I didn't really look. I told Gilvain that I hadn't been able to find it. He was… not pleased. He continued the search himself."

"And did he find it?" I asked.

"Definitely not, or he would have left for Elfame already."

As Con took Thorven away, I was almost sorry we'd solved this particular crime. Almost.

I glanced at Eoinn. Now that Thorven had confessed, he no longer had to worry about being arrested for murder.

I guess I wasn't sorry at all.

nineteen

"It's in the statue, isn't it?"

Branwen stared at me. I'd caught her as she was about to unlock the door to The Cupcake Goddess. "Did you forget your coffee this morning? You're not making sense."

It was stupid early in the morning—in fact, it was still dark out—and I hadn't even gone to bed yet. She had a point. Still, I wasn't letting her off the hook that easily.

"The mirror, Branwen. The one that allows the fae to travel between Elfame and the human realm. It's hidden in the statue." I was sure of it.

"What makes you think it's in the statue?"

"Gilvain was on the hunt for it, and the last place he looked before he died was that statue. He was obsessed with it." Obsessed might be a strong word, but he'd been incredibly eager. I watched him poke and prod the thing. He hadn't found anything, but something in my bones told me it was there.

"Why would anyone hide an object that powerful in plain sight?" she scoffed.

"For just that reason. Because it's in plain sight. No one would suspect a thing."

She shook her head. "That's ridiculous."

"Come on, Branwen. It's time."

Her expression was stubborn. "Time for what?"

"Time to make sure Hefydd and his enforcers will never make it through the veil. At least not in numbers that count."

She shook her head. "This is ridiculous." Nevertheless, she followed me down the street to the roundabout.

Elvira and the rest of the council, along with Quintero, Con, Emerald, the Pixietwists, and several other townsfolk, had all gathered around the gold statue in the center of the roundabout. The statue of Branwen, looking out to sea. One golden hand was outstretched as if to grasp the setting sun. The other?

In the other was an ornate hand mirror. Statue Branwen held it up as if admiring herself. It was so typically the goddess that no one had ever batted an eyelash. Because of course she'd be admiring herself. Nobody had realized that the mirror wasn't just a part of the statue.

I glanced from her to the mirror and back again. I let her see that I knew. That we all did.

"It's been safe there for hundreds of years," Branwen hissed. "Every time we move it, we risk Hefydd discovering its location."

"This time we destroy it." Elvira stepped forward. "It's the only way."

"You think we didn't try that?" Branwen rolled her eyes. "If Belle's magic and mine combined couldn't destroy it, nothing will." She was talking about my ancestor, Isabelle Jones.

"You were drained from creating the town," I pointed out. "Belle probably was too. This time we've got a full council, plus modern technology. Besides, Gilvain figured out where it was. If he could, so could others."

"Fine." She shot me a glare. "I'll need your magic."

I nodded.

She stepped up to the statue and placed her hand on the mirror. I wrapped my hands around the handle, just under hers. I could feel the zing of her magic. Even as limited as it was, she was still more powerful than any being I'd ever met. I let my own magic out to flow with hers.

There was a loud crack and the gold covering the mirror shattered, tiny pieces falling to the ground beneath the statue. The real mirror was revealed, just as gorgeous and ornate as the statue version, but bronze instead of gold. Together we pulled it from statue Branwen's hands.

I let go and, with some reluctance, Branwen handed the mirror to Elvira. "I still don't think it'll work."

Elvira shrugged. "It'll work or it won't. But we must try."

I hated to see something so beautiful destroyed. But Elvira was right. It was the only way to keep us all safe.

"I think it's time," Elvira said. It was early evening, and we were enjoying a drink in the Vault.

I stared at her in consternation. I wasn't ready for this. I'd probably never be ready for this.

It had been a week since the truth about the murder had come out. The witch council had tried to destroy the mirror, but that had, unfortunately, not worked no matter what they tried. Lemon told me they even ran over it with a steamroller. Instead, they'd moved it and hidden it once again. Not even Elvira knew where. Hopefully that would be enough to keep Hefydd at bay. At least for a while.

Since Thorven had killed Gilvain in the defense of another—or, rather, several others if you included the entire town—the council gave him probation and community service. Mostly that involved teaching some of the young people of the town how to do woodworking, since that was a talent of his, and fixing things around town. I was glad for Bellamy's sake that they hadn't thrown him in prison. It was clear to everyone that Thorven would never harm anyone unless his grandchild was threatened. That was something I could understand.

"Are you sure?" I asked Elvira. "The lessons are going well. Lemon said I'm an Elemental Eclectic. Isn't that good enough? Does it really matter where my fire magic comes from?" I had no idea why I was so reluctant, but ever since I found out about the fire magic, I'd had a weird, twitchy feeling.

"It does." Her tone brooked no argument. "Your powers are still unpredictable and difficult to control. If we can figure out exactly where your fire magic comes from, perhaps we can find someone to train you properly."

"If you could just do a spell to figure this out, why didn't you do it before?" I grumbled.

She gave me a stern look. "As I told you before, it takes a very special sort of magic to confirm magical abilities and witch family lines. It's not something I could have done on my own, and until recently, I didn't realize there was someone in town who could help. To that end, I've called in a few friends. Come." She led me out of the Vault and over to one of the sections of the bank she'd designated for spellwork.

The front door swung open and Emerald and Dahlia trooped in. Behind them trailed Lemon. All three wore long, flowing robes in green, pink, and yellow respectively. I guess they'd really gotten into the spirit of things.

"Lemon's not a witch," I said softly as they joined us.

"No, she's not. But she has abilities that will help us, and she's agreed to do so. We need her special brand of magic for this." Louder Elvira said, "Okay, circle everyone. As you know, we're mostly here to figure out where in her background JJ's fire magic comes from, but while we're at it, we're just going to confirm the rest of what Lemon discovered."

Lemon seemed surprisingly cool about having her magic questioned. Not that we were technically questioning it. Except for maybe the fire part. That I wasn't so sure about.

In preparation for the spell, Elvira had already set out two bowls in the center of the area, one filled with various dried herbs and one of crystals in every color of the rainbow. A purple candle was next to the bowls. Fat, white candles were set in even intervals to form a wide circle. The five of us stepped inside the circle formed by the candles and formed a second loose circle.

"Everyone ready?" Elvira asked. Once everyone nodded in the affirmative, she pulled her saltshaker from her track suit pocket and shook out a salt line around the candles before taking up her own spot in the inner circle. "Nothing shall enter, and nothing shall leave. The circle is cast." She clapped her hands and the candle wicks flamed to life.

Elvira leaned down and grabbed the bowl of herbs and the purple candle. She touched the flame of the candle to the dried herbs. There was a flash of flame which almost instantly died down into a wisp of fragrant smoke.

She set the bowl and candle back down, letting the aromatic smoke drift around us, then picked up the bowl of crystals. "Hold out your hands JJ."

I did as she asked, cupping my hands as if to hold water. Elvira placed a pale blue stone in my hand. I felt… nothing.

She smiled. "Aquamarine associated with water magic."

"I don't feel anything."

"Of course not," Lemon said, rolling her eyes. "We already knew you weren't a Water Witch."

"Then why bother?" I asked.

Elvira snorted. "We need a baseline for how you react."

I guess that made sense.

Elvira plucked the aquamarine from my hands and replaced it with a chunk of amethyst. Lemon eyed me carefully as if expecting me to sprout horns. Then her lips quirked knowingly.

I shook my head. "Sorry, nothing."

"Not surprised," Elvira said. "Amethyst is associated with Air. Let's try smoky quartz which is connected to Earth magic."

Turned out I wasn't an Earth Witch, or a Green Witch, nor was I a Storm Witch. Cosmic was a bust, too. Each time Lemon smirked, her eyes sparkling as if to say, "I told you so." But when Elvira put a sunstone in my hand, something sparked. I felt a buzz of energy and the stone glowed gently, bathing my hands in pale orange light.

Lemon grinned. "Like I said, Fire Witch. It's not the main thing, but it's definitely there."

Which explained the exploding coffee pots and the garbage cans catching on fire. I suppose it also explained why my powers were triggered by hot flashes sometimes.

"Let's try fluorite," Elvira said. She placed a gorgeous crystal tower with swirls of green, purple, and white in my hand.

Immediately, the stone flared to life, shooting colored light out into the room. The buzz of magic through me was so strong I almost felt like I'd jump out of my skin.

"Eclectic," Lemon said smugly. "I'm never wrong about these things, Elvira."

"We always have to be certain," Elvira chided gently.

She tried several more crystals, but not one of them flared like the fluorite or even the sunstone. A couple of them felt a little warm or gave a little zing, but it was clear which of the crystals were the winners. Elvira returned both stones to my hands. This time the flare and the zing were brighter than ever.

"Yes, as I said, Eclectic Witch," Lemon confirmed, circling me carefully, her gaze not directly on me but on the air around me. "Fire. Definitely Fire. It's the Eclectic whatsis that makes the Fire unpredictable."

"How is that possible?" Elvira asked. "The Jones line has never produced a Fire Witch. Not in hundreds of years. I checked the records."

Lemon shook her head. "This fire energy isn't of the Jones line. It's something else."

"What does that mean?" I asked.

"Since the Jones blood is on your father's side, and that's where you get your Eclectic powers, I'm going to guess the Fire Witch comes from your mother," Lemon said as if it made perfectly logical sense.

"Plot twist," Dahlia whispered loudly to Emerald.

"That's not possible," I protested. "My mother is completely mundane. Not a magic bone in her body." I could just imagine her face if I told her she was descended from witches.

Lemon shrugged. "I only tell you what I see. And what I see is you've got witch blood on both sides of your lineage. This line?" She traced her finger through the air like she was following a route on a map. "This is the Jones line. Lots of magic in the Jones line, but you got the Elemental." She moved her finger to the other side of my head. "This line isn't as strong, but it's there. And this line is unadulterated fire magic." She gave me a long look. "This is your maternal line."

My heart was pounding so hard I was afraid I might inadvertently blow something up. I took a deep, calming breath and turned to Elvira. "How can that be?" Wouldn't I have known if my mother was a witch? Sure, she was a little odd, but there was nothing inexplicable about her.

"Maybe it's further back," Emerald suggested. "It could have been your great-grandmother or something."

Dahlia nodded. "Like it skipped a generation. That's how it is in my family. Not every woman gets power. My mom doesn't have a magical bone in her body, but my grandmother is a pretty good kitchen witch."

"Oh, no," Lemon said softly. "This magic is much, much closer. It flows through every woman of the line."

"If that were the case, surely my mother would have known. She'd have said something," I protested. I didn't buy it. Not for a minute. I knew my mother didn't have power.

"Are you sure about that?" Elvira said.

"Positive."

"Then I think it's time you called your mother."

Another week had passed since the ritual. I'd rung my mother as Elvira suggested. As usual, there was no answer and it had gone to voicemail. I'd left a barely coherent message. No doubt she'd accuse me of either being drunk or having a nervous breakdown. If she ever called back.

I was up on a stepladder, dusting off the top shelf of books, when the doorbell chimed. "Be right with you." I tucked the handle of my feather duster in my back pocket and climbed down. I turned and froze.

A woman of about seventy stood there, a half-smile on her face. "Hello, Darling. You called?"

I clutched a ladder rung as the room swung around me. Not literally, but it felt that way. "Mom. What are you doing here? How did you get into Miracle Bay?" Only magical people could get in unless they had help. "Did someone let you in? Elvira?"

My mother's expression turned serious. "Juniper, we need to talk."

The End

Want to try Elvira's limoncello cocktail? Keep reading for a delightfully witchy brew...

Did you enjoy Juniper's latest adventure? Want to know more about Miracle Bay and its denizens? Check out the first book in the Season of the Witch paranormal cozy mystery women's fiction series, *Lifestyles of the Witch and Ageless* available at your favorite ebook online retailer.

Sign up to be notified about the next Season of the Witch story, *If the Broom Fits*!

landing.mailerlite.com/webforms/landing/o6t4l3

You can find Shéa on her website **www.sheamacleod.com/ or on Facebook at www.facebook.com/sheamacleodcozymysteries.**

Clarifying Limoncello Lemon Drop

This delightful take on a Moscow Mule is not only perfect for the holidays, but a fun way to bring a little witchy magic into your life.

1 ½ ounce vodka
½ ounce orange liqueur (such as triple sec)
½ to 1 ounce limoncello (depending on how lemony you like it)
1 ounce lemon juice
1 ounce simple syrup (for an extra witchy kick, use *rosemary simple syrup)
Ice

Add all the ingredients to a cocktail shaker and shake well (at least 20 seconds). While you shake, visualize all the negativity washing away and a layer of protection covering you. Imagine any difficult situations becoming clear and every negative thing that comes your way bouncing right off you.

Strain the cocktail into a coupe glass. Garnish with fresh lemon peel.

Enjoy!

Note: If you prefer a non-alcoholic version, simply replace the vodka with an alcohol-free vodka alternative (there are several on the market which can be purchased online) or club soda. Leave out the limoncello and orange liqueur. You can up the lemon juice and simple syrup to your taste.

*Making your own simple syrup is easy! Simply heat one cup of water to a boil, add 1 cup of sugar and stir until the sugar dissolves. For an extra boost of clarity, protection, and purification, drop a sprig or two of fresh rosemary into the hot simple syrup. It will give it a lovely herbal hint that will taste great with the lemon. Once cool, pour the syrup into a glass jar, seal, and store in the fridge up to 30 days!

JJ's Cleansing Honey Lemon Salt Scrub

Wash away negativity and leave your skin super soft with this heavenly smelling salt scrub.

3/4 cup fine sea salt (for protection, purification, and healing)
1/4 cup olive oil (for healing, peace, and protection)
½ teaspoon melted honey, preferably raw (for sweetness and prosperity)
1 Tablespoon lemon juice, preferably fresh squeezed (for longevity, purification, and happiness)
A few drops lemon essential oil (for an extra witchy kick)

Pour salt into a large stainless steel or glass bowl. Add the rest of the ingredients and stir until well mixed. Store in airtight container and use within two weeks.

If you don't have extra fine sea salt, you can use brown sugar!

Use this salt scrub once a week to exfoliate your skin. You can also combine it with a purification shower ritual to get that negativity out of your life!

A Note from Shéa MacLeod

Thank you for reading. If you enjoyed this book, I'd appreciate it if you'd help others find it so they can enjoy it too.

Please return to the site where you purchased this book and leave a review to let other potential readers know what you liked or didn't like about the story.

Book updates can be found at www.sheamacleod.com

Be sure to sign up for my mailing list, so you don't miss out!
landing.mailerlite.com/webforms/landing/o6t4l3

You can follow me on Facebook
www.facebook.com/sheamacleodcozymysteries/ or on Instagram under @SheaMacLeod_Author.

About Shéa MacLeod

Shéa MacLeod is the author of the *Lady Rample Mysteries*, the popular historical cozy mystery series set in 1930s London and the *Deepwood Witches Mysteries,* set in a fictional small town in the modern-day Pacific Northwest. She's also written paranormal romance and mysteries, urban fantasy, and contemporary romances with a splash of humor. She resides in the leafy green hills outside Portland, Oregon, where she indulges her fondness for strong coffee, *Murder, She Wrote* reruns, cocktails, and dragons.

Because everything's better with dragons.

Other Books by Shéa MacLeod

Season of the Witch
(A Paranormal Women's Fiction Cozy Mystery)
Lifestyles of the Witch and Ageless
In Charm's Way
Witchmas Spirits
Battle of the Hexes
If the Broom Fits (coming soon)

Edwina Gale Paranormal Investigator
(A Paranormal Women's Fiction Cozy Mystery)
Day of the Were-Jackal (coming spring 2022)
Night of the Conjurer (coming summer/fall 2022)

Deepwood Witches Mysteries
(A Paranormal Cozy Mystery)
Potions, Poisons, and Peril
Wisteria, Witchery, and Woe
Moonlight, Magic, and Murder
Dreams, Divination, and Danger
Alchemy, Arsenic, and Alibis
Crystals, Cauldrons, and Crime

Viola Roberts Cozy Mysteries
(Contemporary Cozy Mysteries)
The Corpse in the Cabana
The Stiff in the Study
The Poison in the Pudding
The Body in the Bathtub
The Venom in the Valentine
The Remains in the Rectory
The Death in the Drink

The Victim in the Vineyard
The Ghost in the Graveyard
The Larceny in the Luau

Lady Rample Mysteries (1930s Cozy Mysteries)
Lady Rample Steps Out
Lady Rample Spies a Clue
Lady Rample and the Silver Screen
Lady Rample Sits In
Lady Rample and the Ghost of Christmas Past
Lady Rample and Cupid's Kiss
Lady Rample and the Mysterious Mr. Singh
Lady Rample and the Haunted Manor
Lady Rample and the Parisian Affair
Lady Rample and the Yuletide Caper
Lady Rample and the Mystery at the Museum (coming soon)

Sugar Martin Vintage Cozy Mysteries
A Death in Devon
A Grave Gala
A Christmas Caper
A Riviera Rendezvous

Printed in Great Britain
by Amazon